MW01328342

# The Mystery of Spooky Hollow

Dexter Williams

Bloomington, IN

Milton Keynes, UK

*AuthorHouse™*
*1663 Liberty Drive, Suite 200*
*Bloomington, IN 47403*
*www.authorhouse.com*
*Phone: 1-800-839-8640*

*AuthorHouse™ UK Ltd.*
*500 Avebury Boulevard*
*Central Milton Keynes, MK9 2BE*
*www.authorhouse.co.uk*
*Phone: 08001974150*



*First published by AuthorHouse 4/5/2006*

*ISBN: 1-4259-2507-3 (sc)*

*Printed in the United States of America*
*Bloomington, Indiana*

*This book is printed on acid-free paper.*

To My Little Furry Baby who i miss so much. Garfield you will always be in my heart, Keep Granddad company for me and I will never forget you. I love you Garfers.

# Table of Contents

# The Mystery of Spooky Hallow

# Chapter One

## A death in the family

It was a sunny June day when Maddox Lewis received the call that would change his life forever.

"Hey, Hey dad throw the ball to me, you're hogging it."

"I'm not hogging it, I'm just throwing it to your brother because you can't catch" said Maddox, then he laughed.

"Ha, Ha, Ha" said Maddox's daughter Misty.

Maddox Lewis was a tall man around 6ft 5in. He was 45 years old and owned a big house in Spruce Creek Fly-in which was located in South Daytona, Florida. Due to the fact that he was a lawyer he had quite a lot of money but he had worked hard for it and had never asked his billionaire father for a dime. But little did he know that in a few short hours he himself would be a billionaire. Every Saturday Maddox and his family would play volley ball in the swimming pool.

It was kind of a tradition, and that's exactly what they were doing when Maddox received the phone call.

"Mr. Lewis there is a phone call for you it's your mother, she said that it's urgent" said Christina the maid.

"Tell her I will be right there" he said as he got out of the pool. He wrapped himself in his black and white towel and sat down on the lounger next to the outside phone.

"Hello Mother" said Maddox.

"Darling I have some very bad news to tell you." Rita said through sobs "Your father has had a heart attack. He was rushed to Dallas Memorial Hospital late last night, he didn't pull through."

There was a long pause "are you alright Mother?" Maddox asked with a quiver in his voice.

"I guess I will be in time, but for now I need you to come to Texas for the reading of the will." said Rita.

"Alright I will be there as soon as possible."

Maddox put the phone down and turned to his wife Suzy who had just gotten out of the pool. Suzy was a short woman with a kind face and eyes that would make anyone feel safe and loved.

"What's happened" she asked as she saw the deep remorseful look that his face now showed. Maddox opened his mouth but only managed two words. "Dads dead" and with that he went through the double French doors into the house.

The next morning when he woke, the initial shock had sunk in and his grief was beyond tears.

"I blame myself for this. I wasn't even there to say goodbye and to be with mother when she needed me the most." He told Suzy.

"It's not your fault, these things are unpredictable." She replied as she hugged her husband.

"When are you going to tell the children?" asked Maddox.

"When you are in Texas, or when they ask where you are going, whichever comes first."

Maddox left for Texas on Monday afternoon and when Misty and Paul asked where their Dad was going Suzy thought now might be a good time to tell them. She sat them down in the lounge and thought for a second how she was going to put the news into words that wouldn't seem too strong for two young children.

"This is not going to be an easy thing to tell you but" she paused "Grandad Williams has left to go and see the Angels and daddy has had to go and see Granny Rita."

Misty and Paul just stood there and then without warning burst into tears.

On the flight to Texas, he thought of all the things that he and his father had done together throughout the years and also how hard he had worked to get the empire that he owned.

As Maddox walked through the airport he saw his mother standing by the exit. Rita looked very well for her age. She was 5ft 2in and had red hair. Maddox gave her a kiss and a hug, together they walked outside. The Chauffeur opened the door to the limousine and they got in.

"Are you ok mum?"

"I guess I will be in time but everything seems so vivid and painful. Lets get this over with I want to go home, Tony take us to George's Law Offices"

"Yes Mam" The chauffeur replied.

They set off towards the lawyer's office but the express way was like a parking lot at 6.00 o'clock on a Monday night.

They finally pulled into the car park at the Lawyers office at 7.30 pm and on a normal occasion they would find the offices closed but as George Lincoln was a good friend of Maddox's father he had said he would stay open, after all it was the least that he could do. Rita and Maddox didn't say anything as they walked through the empty building. When they got to the door that read, George Lincoln, Maddox knocked three times. They heard a faint "Come in" and they entered the darkened room.

"Thank you for coming. I am so sorry to hear about your father Maddox, he was a great man" George said. He sat on his high backed leather chair behind his desk. The room was quite small and had a settee in one corner and a liquor cupboard in the other, its dark oak panelling gave the office a homely feel, a fire crackled away in the grate of a stone fireplace.

"Before we begin" said Maddox "don't you think that my brother and sister should be here?"

"There is no need, your father wrote a covering letter to explain his wishes, and the actual will is the legal side of it. I will read it to you.

*"My darling wife and sons, if you are hearing this letter I am no longer with you. This has not been an easy letter to write and perhaps you won't understand some of my reasons, and for that I am sorry. I am going to leave the Lewis mansion and its contents to my darling wife Rita along with $10 million. I am sure this will be enough to support you for the rest of your life.*

*Maddox I am leaving you Lewis Oil Co and the rest Lewis fortune use it well. Ronald I leave you nothing for this you know my reasons.*

*Samantha. If you think you deserve anything your worse than I thought. After what you have put this family through you are lucky that I have even acknowledged you.*

*I love you all very much, be happy. I will always be with you."*

*William Lewis.*

# Chapter Two

## The Billions

Maddox sat in the leather seat in George Lincoln's Office just staring out of the tall window behind the desk, not daring to believe what he had just heard.

"There must be some mistake, he couldn't have left Lewis Oil Co to me and nothing to my brother I thought they had cleared that issue up years ago." Maddox stuttered.

"As I said before the cover letter is to explain his wishes the actual will is just a formality. Lewis Oil Co will be in your name by the end of the week and $10 million will be transferred into Mrs. Lewis's account by tomorrow, the remainder of the fortune will be transferred into your account by Thursday. The Fortune as it stands to day is in excess of $4 billion. If you have any questions please don't hesitate to ask me." George said.

"Thank you George, I dare say you will be in contact to finalize the remainder of the will, now Maddox if you don't mind I would like to get home as I am very tired." Rita said as she got out of her seat very shakily.

They said goodbye to George and left the building. As they got into the limousine and set of toward Rita's house Maddox turned to his mother.

"I thought Ronald and father cleared their issues up a long time ago. Father told me that he had a chat with Ronald at my 20th Birthday Party."

"That's what he told you. He never spoke to Ronald and when he tried to, Ronald just threw it back in his face and wouldn't have anything more to do with him. That is why he cut him out of his will. He said that Ronald would have to contact him and mend the bridges, but he never did which is something your father regretted until the end of his days." Tears formed in her eyes and she took out a handkerchief and wiped them away, she turned to face out of the window. Maddox could see that their conversation was over. When he arrived at the mansion that he had grown up in, he was suddenly filled with a sorrow that he could not explain. He opened the great oak doors so that his mother could enter the cavernous entrance hall. Directly in front of the doors was a magnificent marble staircase, which spiralled its way to the upper three floors. Maddox hadn't been back to the mansion for a long time but he didn't recall having the empty feeling that he now felt as he stood there in the entrance hall. He suspected the reason was that his father was no longer present. William seemed to fill the house with a certain warmth and fullness that made you feel welcome and wanted.

Maddox stayed in Texas until the will was finalized and the papers were signed to recognize him as the new owner of Lewis Industries, which included Lewis Oil Co and the Lewis fortune.

After a week in Texas, Maddox decided it was time to return home to his family.

"You take care won't you and bring the kids and Suzy to Texas to see me. I would like to see Misty and Paul more often now that they are growing up so fast. Paul being 7 and Misty being 6 the time fly's by so quickly, life's short on this earth we need to live it to the full each and everyday." Rita told Maddox as he was about to board the Lewis Company Jet.

"I will, you take care if you need anything just pick up the phone and call me and I'll get on the jet and come straight over." He replied as he gave her a hug.

"Oh I wish all my children were as kind as you. Ronald never keeps in contact and Samantha.... Well that's another matter, anyway you take care."

"I think we will be hearing from Samantha very soon especially as I am now the new owner of Lewis Industries. Bear in mind what

I said about calling me and feel free to come and visit me in Florida, especially in the winter as it gets so cold here. Take care mother."

"I will" She gave her son another hug and waved goodbye as he climbed the stairs to the jet.

The doors closed, the engines roared and he was gone. Rita got back into the limousine, wondering what was left in her life.

Maddox landed at Orlando airport and made his way to the car park. He collected his car and drove up to the barrier. He paid his parking ticket which came to $40.00 and drove off. On the way home he was thinking of how he was going to tell his wife and children what he had inherited. More over he was thinking of what would happen when he told his brother that he had been left nothing and that Maddox had been left everything. He thought he had better make that stop first. Exiting the interstate he saw the sign post for DeLand and braced himself for what was about to come.

He knocked on the door and Debbie, Ronald's wife answered.

"He's in the lounge; Your Mother just called and told him about your father." She said miserably.

"Did she tell him about the reading of the will?" he asked.

"No she didn't." she replied.

Maddox walked into the Lounge and saw his brother sitting in the chair with beer bottles surrounding him.

"Ronald" Maddox said.

He made a slight grunting noise to indicate that he was listening.

"I've been in Texas for the reading of the will and Father has left everything to me and mother. I'm sorry."

Ronald sat bolt upright and started yelling in a drunken stupor.

"Get Out" he said so menacingly Maddox actually felt apprehensive. He started throwing beer bottles at his brother "I never want to see or speak to you again. GET OUT." He yelled.

"But Ronald it's not....." Maddox begun but when the second beer bottle missed his head by about eighth of an inch he thought he had better leave or he would have to go to hospital and have the shards of glass from the Michelob bottle removed from his skull.

Maddox left the house his worst fears confirmed. His brother blamed him for his father's decision. Although he and his brother had never been close he couldn't help feel a certain sadness.

He got into his car and drove off. An ever growing lump of guilt in his throat.

"You're kidding me" Suzy said when he told her about the reading.

"No I'm not kidding you. I stopped by Ronald's house on the way home and he threw beer bottles at me and told me that he never wanted to see or speak to me again. I think it was just a spur of the moment thing but you never can tell with him."

"Daddy does this mean that we don't have to go to school again?" Misty asked her Father.

"I'm afraid you still have to go to school." He replied smiling.

Maddox turned to his wife "I am going to have to call my lawyer and tell him what has happened so he can set up a trust fund for the kids." Suzy agreed that it was a good idea. Maddox went to bed early that night as he had a lot to think over. One of the things was what he was going to say to his sister when she got in contact with him. Now that he owned a $4 billion empire, he didn't think it would be too long.

# Chapter Three.

# Maddox's New Car and Doxam International Airways

The next few days were very busy for Maddox due to the fact that his lawyer was pressuring him into investing his money. Suzy couldn't under stand why Maddox needed a lawyer as he was one himself but his reply was "well he's an old friend and if my idea takes off I won't have time to manage my money. This puzzled Suzy slightly but she forgot about it soon after.

"I really think that you should invest at least some of your money so you have something to show for it, as it stands now your money is in the bank doing nothing." David Cornish, Maddox's lawyer said.

"I already have plans for some of the money. I want to buy an airline and an abandoned quarry if I can find one." He said as they were sitting in David's office.

"Ok, but why on earth do you want a quarry?"

"Because I am going to turn it into a theme park."

"That's a good idea." said David who sounded as enthusiastic as Maddox did.

"I have already seen the airline that I want to buy it is going into receivership so we should be able to get it pretty cheap. Then we will need to buy new planes. We will need to get someone to design the rides for the theme park which I am going to call Spooky Hollow and I have the perfect person to do it. If he will agree to talk to me. I think I'll call the airline Doxam international." Maddox said.

"Sounds like you have it all planned out. Well I'll get my people on to finding you an old quarry and if you will phone me with the details of the Airline I will get the wheels in motion for the purchase." David said.

Maddox was really looking forward to doing something worth while and the fact that he would be giving families somewhere to go and have a safe enjoyable time. When he told his wife what he was going to do she was really surprised but agreed to help him think of some rides to build. Maddox thought he had better get in contact with the person that he wanted to build the rides. So once again found himself outside his brother's house. He knocked on the door twice and this time Ronald opened it, but before Maddox could say anything Ronald said

"I'm sorry about the other day Maddox I think it was the shock of you telling me that father had left everything to you and the fact that I was drunk at the time, after all it's not your fault."

Maddox was slightly taken aback at the abrupt attitude change. He wondered why his brother had changed his mind so quickly. In fact it sent a chill down his spine, but he dismissed it.

"No it's not my fault but I have something for you to do for me and if you will consent to do it I will make you a very rich man."

"Come in and we'll talk about it."

Maddox followed his brother into the small living room and pulled out a seat from the under the table.

"Beer?" Ronald asked.

"No thanks."

"Suit yourself. Ok now what was it you were saying?"

"I'm going to build a theme park and I was wondering if you'd design and build it for me.

"Wow, yes I will do that for you." He replied with a smile on his face.

"I will pay you $10 million. That sound ok?" he asked. Ronald just grinned.

Maddox stayed for a while and chatted about thoughts for rides before deciding that he would go and buy himself a new car. However he didn't tell his brother what he was going to do as he thought it might upset him. He said goodbye to Ronald and headed for the Porsche garage in downtown Orlando.

As Maddox pulled into the Garage and got out of his car a sales man came running over to him. Maddox was strongly reminded of a Cheetah approaching his prey.

"Can I help you?" Asked the sales man.

"Yes I would like to buy a new car." But just as Maddox had said 'new car' there was a loud bang behind him and when he turned round he saw that the exhaust pipe was hanging off his Civic.

"Ah" said Maddox "Right well let's go and look at the cars then shall we?" Maddox set off toward the building with the sales man in tow. However he looked some what more subdued than when Maddox first said he wanted to buy a car. Maybe it was the fact that he thought Maddox was just having him on and he wasn't going to get the commission.

"How much is this one?" Maddox asked as he pointed to a Blood red convertible 911 Carrera.

"It's very expensive" Maddox detected a slight emphasis on the word very.

"Listen" Said Maddox now getting slightly agitated that the sales man didn't think that he was genuine "I am hear to buy a high performance car and if you don't want to deal with me then that's fine. I will take my custom elsewhere."

Maddox turned and left thinking I'll show him'. He pulled off the remaining piece of his exhaust pipe and threw it into the middle of the car park. He sped down I-4 the sound of the exhaust-less civic made Maddox feel like a boy racer. He dismissed the thought thinking that he would feel much better when he had the car that he was on a mission to acquire. The 'Boy Racer' exited the interstate. He drove down the road for quite some time until he saw a Bank of America. After finding a parking space in the packed car park Maddox went into the building and got in the queue to see a teller. There was an elderly man in front of him who insisted that the teller gave him his pension in one dollar bills. Maddox was beginning to get a bit frustrated and just as he was about to leave and go and find a less crowded bank, another teller opened up a spot and beckoned him over.

"How can I help you" said the teller who was a young and very attractive blonde.

"I would like to withdraw $300,000 out of this account" he handed the women his check card. "And I would like the aforementioned amount to be in a cashiers check made out to Orlando Ferrari."

The teller looked slightly taken a back that a man has just asked her for $300,000 out of his checking account. However she took Maddox's card and said

"We will have to run a security check first which will take about ten minutes so if you would like to take a seat over there by the door" she pointed to three vacant seats upholstered in green suede "I will call you over when we have received the all clear."

Maddox went over to the seats and sat down on the one nearest the door. He picked up a magazine from the table and began to read an article about the advances that the new Palm Pilot Tungsten E had.

After what seemed about half an hour, but was really twelve minutes, the teller waved him over.

"We have been given the all clear; hear is your check, if you could just sign the bottom you will be ready to go."

Maddox signed the bottom of the check and the teller tore off the copy that was needed for bank records. She gave Maddox the check and his card and said,

"Have a nice day Mr. Lewis."

"You too" he replied.

He left the bank, got back into his 'Fart Box' civic and sped off down the road. Back onto the Interstate he dodged the cars that were trying to pass him. He even heard a horn being pipped at him but when the driver of the offending civic saw that it was a grown man driving the car and not a teenager he sped of at top speed only to get pulled over by a state trooper who was in the lane beside Maddox. Maddox chuckled to himself when he looked into the rear view mirror and saw the officer get out of his Chevy Camero and walk up to the teenager's car. Maddox took the exit to the Ferrari & Maserati garage and screeched to a halt outside the main office building. 'Here we go again' thought Maddox seeing the sales man hurrying over to his prospective customer.

Maddox got out of his car and heard the sales man say

"Can" but before he could finish his sentence Maddox said

"Yes you can help me. I would like to purchase a new car, and" Maddox put his hand into his inside left jacket pocket and pulled out the freshly printed check. "Hear is the money for the car that I wish to purchase."

The sale man who was about 5ft tall and dumpy stood flabbergasted.

"Right well lets go and look at the cars then shall we? My name is Colin by the way"

"Maddox Lewis" Maddox replied.

They went over to the showroom and Colin held open the door so that Maddox could go in a head and get the WOW factor.

"That one" said Maddox immediately. He pointed to a blue Spyder convertible.

"Excellent choice Mr. Lewis. Well if you're sure, why don't we step into my office and sort out the paper work." Maddox followed the man through a door to the right of the one that they had come in from. They walked down a hallway that was lined with pictures of different model Ferraris. Colin led Maddox into a small room off to the right of the main corridor.

"Have a seat and make yourself comfortable. I will be right back with the paperwork that will need to be signed. Would you like a coffee?"

"No thank you" replied Maddox.

The door closed and he was left alone. He started visually exploring the room. First to catch his eye was the poster size pictures of a Ferrari Testerosa glinting in the evening sun. He then saw a picture of Colin holding a baby and a tall black haired women standing next to him.

This could only be Colin's family. Just as Maddox was looking at the picture on the wall over the filing cabinet the door opened and Colin returned, clutching a folder.

"Ok. I have pre filled out the paper work all you need to do is provide me with your insurance details so we can get your new car ready to go. I will also need to see your drivers licence. Oh and what do you want to do with your old car?"

Maddox handed over his driving licence and said

"You can have the car along with whatever is left from that cashiers check I gave you."

Once again Colin was extremely surprised.

"Why thank you Mr. Lewis"

"Maddox"

"Thank you Maddox" Maddox gave Colin the information on the insurance company and he phoned it through.

After about five minutes Colin said

"Your tag will come by mail in about four weeks, well that's it, your ready to go here are your keys" he handed Maddox the keys to his new car "and you have a good afternoon sir."

"That was really fast" Maddox said "Are you always this efficient?"

"Well we aim to please" he replied "have a good afternoon"

Maddox left through the main office door this time instead of going back through the showroom. When he walked out of the office building he saw his new car sitting in a car park space reflecting the sun. The roof was down and he couldn't wait to get in.

On the way home a guy in a Mercedes tailed him for three junctions and in the end he got fed up with it. Maddox slipped his new car down a gear and punched the accelerator. He left the guy for dust. Maddox pulled up outside his home, all the neighbours staring at his new automobile. Anyhow Maddox never did get on well with the neighbours. They were the type that looked over each others fences to compare the neatness of their grass. "I really must think about moving." He thought.

Maddox hardly had time to sit down over the next few days as his lawyer had found him a quarry and had purchased the airline and 10 new planes, which had all been fitted out with leather seats and play stations for children on long flights. Ronald had begun designing the rides for the theme park and ringing contractors to request bids for the massive amount of work needed to bring Maddox's dreams of a wonderful ghost orientated theme park to reality.

It was July 4th 2002 and Maddox was standing in his bedroom in front of the mirror trying to tie his tie.

"Not long now" Suzy said to her husband bustling over to him and pushing his hands out of the way "Maddox you are 40 years old I would have thought by now you would be able to tie a tie properly."

"Well we can't all be as talented as you can we darling." They looked at each other and burst out laughing.

The door opened and in came Misty and Paul in their best clothes.

"Daddy if you want to be on time for the launch of your new airline we had better go now." Said Misty.

Maddox passed a set of keys to his wife. The main key had a big H on it. He then passed a silver key to Paul.

"Go and open the inside Garage door please. Misty go with your brother. Suzy come with me." Taking his wife by the hand they followed their children down the spiral oak staircase towards the garage.

"Maddox what have you bought now?" Suzy asked her husband interestingly.

They reached the closed garage door.

"Ok Paul open it." Maddox told his son.

He put the key in the lock and turned it. The door sprang open. There in the middle of the Garage stood a brand new shiny black Hummer with leather interior and Television sets with separate DVD players in the back.

"OH MY GOSH" Suzy yelled with delight "I can't believe it. Thank you so much." She flung her arms around her husband, then pulled away and got into her new Hummer H2. The two children got into the back and Maddox got into the Passenger seat.

"Right we'd better go or we will be late and darling although it's a V8 Please keep it below 90." Said Maddox. Suzy laughed. Maddox pushed the button to open the automatic garage door, which was integrated into the sun visor, and they reversed out onto the road.

They sped down I-4 to Orlando airport where the launch of Doxam international would be. They arrived 10 minutes late and as Suzy slammed on the brakes in the executive parking space Labelled Maddox Lewis there was an intake of breath from the back seat and Paul said

"Are all those planes yours daddy?" As he looked out of the window and saw the 10 sparkling new Boeing 747's lined up just waiting for a cargo and some passengers.

"Yes son they are."

They got out of the car and practically ran toward the entrance to the airport.

There was around 50 People standing in Front of the check in desk waiting for Maddox to cut the red tape to officially open Doxam international.

"Friends and family." He said "the cutting of this tape marks the beginning of a dream. A dream that will be carried on by my children and their children after them. Ladies and Gentlemen I give you Doxam International" he cut the tape and as he did so the lights behind the desk were turned on and the staff came out of a door to the right and took their seats behind their new desks. There were people whistling and cheering as they stood watching Maddox Lewis smiling and shaking people's hands. He had done it. Phase one of his dream was complete.

# Chapter Four.

## Samantha

Two weeks after the launch of Doxam International the plans for Spooky Hollow were ready and the contractors were lined up to begin the work. The Scheduled date of opening was July 4th 2004 that gave them 24 months to get the park built and ready, to welcome its first excited park guests.

"Maddox Lewis industries." Said Lisa the secretary.

"I would like to speak to Maddox Lewis please." Said the female voice.

"Who shall I say is calling?" asked Lisa.

"His Sister." Replied the voice

"One moment please.

Maddox was sitting in his office on the top floor of his new Lewis Oil Company headquarters building in Orlando behind his leather desk. Although it had the best view, Maddox's office wasn't; the biggest in the building. It had a couple of pictures on the wall, which included his family. There were three chairs in front of his desk. Some people may have argued, why three seats? Well the truth was that Maddox Lewis had found that when he was a kid, any office building that he went into with his parents only had two chairs which left Maddox standing. He didn't want that to happen when people came to see him with their children in toe. Maddox heard the secretarial intercom beep so he pressed the button which allowed him to speak to Lisa and said,

"Yes" said Maddox.

"There's a call for you on line 3. She says it's your sister." Said Lisa.

"Thank you Lisa" replied Maddox. "Here we go." He said to himself.

He pushed the button to allow the call on line three to his telephone.

"Well Samantha I must admit that I am surprised it has taken you so long." Said Maddox.

"Oh believe me darling brother it wouldn't have if I could have found the number sooner. I want to see you today." Samantha demanded.

Samantha was the eldest child of the Lewis family. Maddox, Ronald, Rita and William had not spoken to Samantha in 20 years. Samantha had run off with her boyfriend when she was 25 because her mother and father had forbidden her to marry him. Daniel, Samantha's boyfriend had been into drugs, car racing and almost any other foul natured thing you could think of. Samantha however didn't think this was a problem. One night she had packed her bags and left. She didn't leave a note to say where she had gone or why. Everyone knew why she had left; it was no secret that she hated her parents but loved their money. Her father had spent 3 years trying to find her and get her to come back home to Texas. He eventually found her living in a hostel in Australia with Daniel. He tried to persuade her to come home with him without Daniel but she had refused. She had most probably read about the death of her father in the news paper as he was so widely known and now she was probably calling to get her hands on some of the Lewis Billions.

"If you want to see me you'll have to come to my office in Orlando I haven't got time to go gallivanting all over the place to meet family members that I haven't seen in years." replied Maddox.

"Fine I'll be there in an hour."

"Oh you're in town then?" he asked.

"Maddox I have been in town for the last 2 weeks. I'll be there in 1 hour. You had better be ready." She said

"Don't you worry. I will be." He said with the same malice his sister had.

With that she hung up. Maddox beeped his secretary.

"Lisa could you come in for a second I need to have a word."

The doors to Maddox's office opened and in came Lisa.

"Yes boss" she said.

"Lisa I need you to double the security and turn on the video surveillance recorders when a brown haired woman comes into the building. She is about 6ft tall and if she hasn't got contacts she will be wearing glasses. If you see the emergency light illuminate on your panel call the security in ok"

"Yes Maddox I will do that. Is there something wrong if you don't mind me asking?"

"Well there could be. My sister can be a very demanding woman when she wants to be. Last time I had an altercation with her I almost got shot. That is one thing I don't want happening again." said Maddox.

Lisa left and Maddox wondered if he should go and get a bullet proof jacket. Then he said to himself "I'm being stupid. She probably only wants a chat." Though he very much doubted it.

Maddox sat back behind his desk and tried to resume his paper work but couldn't. He was too busy wondering what his sister wanted. He thought he knew but he just wasn't quite sure. However he didn't have to wait long because trouble came early.

Samantha Lewis stormed through the doors to the main office, completely ignoring Lisa who said "Can I help you" and headed for the big oak door that held a plaque saying Maddox Lewis (President). She pushed it open and strode into her brothers office.

"Hello Samantha." Said Maddox not bothering to rise from his desk to greet his sibling. "Long time no see. How's Daniel?" he asked sarcastically.

"Oh that's been over for years he died of an overdose. Still I got lucky, turned out he had rich parents that died and left him a bit of money, it came to me when he died. We both know why I'm here so lets just cut to the chase shall we?"

"Yes please do I have import things to attend to."

"As you have inherited a majority of the Lewis fortune and our brother and I got nothing perhaps you would like to give your old sister a bit."

"Ah" Maddox said. "I thought that might be what it was. You heard that I got the Lewis Fortune and you thought you would come and take a chunk of it did you? Well I've got news for you sis. It's been 20 years and no phone call, no letter or anything. You didn't even have the generosity to call our mother to ask her if she was alright or if she needed anything after father died did you? You didn't call me or Ronald to find out if we were ok. All you care about is money and Samantha Lewis and I will die before I let you have one dime of

Father's money. Your nothing but slime now get out of my office before I have you thrown out."

"Not until you sign over 1 third of the company to me."

"What are you on you stupid bitch. GET OUT" yelled Maddox. He was now standing yelling at the top of his lungs at his sister. Maddox Lewis was not a person you wanted to get in the way of when he was in a bad temper.

He had had enough. He pressed the button on his intercom for Lisa to send in the security guards.

The doors opened and in came two guards built like bodybuilders.

"Gentlemen remove this woman" said Maddox calmly.

They each took her by an arm and led her towards the door, but she didn't go quietly.

"I'll get you for this Maddox" she screeched as she was dragged out of the door "I'll bring Maddox Industries, Doxam International and Spooky Hollow crashing down around your ears."

"Wait" he told the guards "How do you know about Spooky Hollow?" Maddox asked.

"I know everything about you Maddox just you wait. I'll ruin you"

BANG. The door to his office slammed shut. He sat wondering how his dratted sister knew about his plans for Spooky Hollow, but in the end he gave up. He wasn't worried after all she was a woman. What did women know?

# Chapter Five

# The Grand Opening

Maddox had not heard from his sister since she had come into his office almost 15 months before, which he hoped could only be a good sign. He and his family were getting really excited as the opening of Spooky Hollow drew closer and closer. It had been 16 and a half months since the plans were drawn up and the workers were contracted. Now everything was almost ready. The rides were practically finished and the pathways and ticket booths just needed to be painted. People had been buying advanced tickets for the grand opening and business men from around the world wanted to become partners in this fantastic empire.

"There is a man from China that wants to become deputy chairman" Maddox told his wife one evening at the dinner table. "But I have decided that I am not going to accept any partners, I am going to keep Spooky Hollow a family owned theme park. I want to be in charge all the time and not have other people telling me what to do, not to mention the fact that I want it to be passed down through the family."

"I think that is a good idea" replied Suzy as she took her husband's empty plate away and put it into the dishwasher. Later that evening as Suzy was sitting out on the front porch swaying back and forth on the swing thinking back to that fateful day when she was almost killed by her manic sister.

It was a cold snowy Ohio day and Suzy was sitting on her bed reading her favourite fairy tale book 'The Lion The Witch and The Wardrobe' for about the sixth time that week, when her sister came in. Suzy looked up from her book and said,

"Hello Veronica, what are you doing?"

"I'm about to kill you" she replied. Suzy laughed, but soon stopped when Veronica pulled out a knife from her pocket and held it over Suzy. Suzy screamed "MUM HELPPPPP" Veronica drove the knife into Suzy's chest just as their mum came running in the door. "SUZY"

The adult Suzy woke up from her doze, not aware that she had fallen asleep. She rubbed her chest where the knife wound scar was still visible. Luckily the knife had not struck any major organs.

Veronica had been sent off to a school in Switzerland for mentally unstable children. Suzy hadn't heard from her since the day that she had almost lost her life. Suzy got up from the swing and went back inside. She had not had the 'Death Dream' as her and Maddox called it for a long time and the fact that it was now making an appearance so close to the opening of Spooky Hollow Made her feel uneasy.

Maddox woke up every hour on the eve of the launch of Spooky Hollow and in the end at 5.00 am he thought to himself that enough is enough. He got up and went into the bathroom, got in the shower and turned it on as cold as it would go.

After drying off, he picked out his best suit and went downstairs to the kitchen and made himself a cup of strong hot coffee. As he sat in the living room staring at the blank wall above the fireplace, he thought he would watch TV but as he put it on there was an advert for Spooky Hollow showing.

"God my hair looks awful" he said under his breath.

At 8.00 am he went to wake up his other family members who seemed to have had a far less restless night than he had. They had breakfast and then made their way down I-4 to Spooky Hollow. When they pulled into the new parking lot, Maddox was amazed to see that the 10,000 parking spaces all seemed to be filled. When he eventually found a space and had parked, he and his family got out and headed over to the entrance where there were thousands upon thousands of people queuing to get in.

Maddox, Suzy, Paul and Misty fought their way to the front accompanied by two security guards and climbed up onto the temporary stage that had been erected next to the Big Black gates. One had a huge S on it, the other had a huge H.

"Ladies and Gentlemen boys and girls, it is with great pleasure and pride that I announce the completion of Spooky Hollow. It has always been my dream to have my own theme park and now that dream has become a reality. I hope that you and your families will enjoy today and return again and again to experience the many rides and attractions we have to offer in this unique adventure. So as I cut the ribbon to open the park I wish you all a fun filled and exciting day." He cut the ribbon and the gates swung open. Everybody cheered and clapped. It was like a heard of stampeding elephants charging into the park. The rest of the day Maddox and his family spent walking around talking to people and asking them what they thought of the park and its rides. Everyone they spoke to said it was one of the best places they had ever been. Maddox knew he had a big hit on his hands.

Misty and Paul wanted to go on the ghost train ride so Maddox and Suzy said goodbye to the people that they were talking to at the time and made their way towards the ride. The ghost train ride consisted of guests getting onto an old mine cart they were then led through a little abandoned village with ghostly noises and things that popped out of the building windows. Then guests were told that the noises and ghostly spirits were "the old miners" they were then hurtled through the underground mine shafts of the old quarry, where they were thrown down a drop of 100ft, forced back up and out of the tunnel and onto the ride entrance.

They used their passes to get to the front of the line and as they were about to board the mine cart Suzy had a sudden change of heart.

"I don't think I actually want to go on this ride Maddox" she said as she read the sign that explained what would be coming in the ride.

"Oh mum don't be such a wimp, come on it will be fine" Paul said to her as the cart pulled into its station. They got into the cart and the hard lap bar came down.

"I really don't want to" Suzy begun but the rest of her words were drowned by the train as it had started to thunder along it's tracks down a little tunnel. They slowed down as they entered the old mining town, everything was quiet and still, then all of a sudden a ghost popped out from a hole in the ceiling right above Suzy's head. She screamed and made the people in the cart in front turn round! They carried on their journey through the abandoned town. Suzy was confronted with 3 more ghosts and by the time that they got off the ride and went outside into the light she was ashen faced and shaking all over.

"Mummy, Mummy what's the matter" Misty asked her mother as she caught sight of her mother's face that she was trying so hard to hide.

"I hate ghosts" she mumbled just loud enough for her husband to hear.

They made their way to the park exit. Suzy was looking really ill.

"Daddy I don't want to go home yet we've only just got here." Paul said

"Paul I own the place we can come back" he said.

Paul caught the look on his fathers face and he knew that it would be no good pursuing the matter.

# Chapter Six

## The First Disappearance

When the Peabody family woke at 8.00 am on the morning of their park adventure they did not think that anything strange, mysterious or upsetting would be coming their way. Simon and Joanne Peabody showered and dressed then went to wake their two children up. TJ their daughter was 13 with long silvery blonde hair and their son Luke who was 15 had black hair with a pony tail. When Joanne and Simon knocked on their doors they found that the children were already awake talking in low hushed voices.

"I want to go on the ghost train ride" said Luke to his sister.

"Yes that looks really good I think I would like to go on there too." She replied and they both laughed.

Joanne and Simon went in and found them huddled over a brochure that had Spooky Hollow written above a drawing of an old village. The parks motto "Where chills will turn your blood to ice" was at the bottom of the brochure in a ghostly looking font.

"Come on you two we need to get going if we are going to get there for when the park opens." Simon said to his children.

They quickly changed from their pyjamas and hurried down stairs, both of them too excited to eat any breakfast. Rufus, the family dog was running around the kitchen barking madly and chasing his tail. It was all getting too much for Joanne who had a horrendous headache due to all the noise and commotion.

"QUIET" she yelled and everybody stopped what they were doing including Rufus who was jumping up at the table to get to the toast Joanne had put there minutes before the children had come down. "Thank you, right TJ please can you take the cooler and put it in the truck. Luke please feed Rufus and Simon go and get into the truck."

Everybody did as they were told and the noise died down to an almost eerie level.

Joanne set the alarm and locked the house before getting into their blue Ford Expedition.

"Right" said Simon. "Spooky Hollow here we come."

They reversed out of the drive and got onto the interstate heading for Kissimmee. Luke and TJ watched 'The Lion King' on the in car DVD player and Simon and Joanne talked about work. Upon arriving they found the signposts for Spooky Hollow. As they drew nearer to the entrance Joanne and Simon could hear the constant chattering from the children in the back.

After buying the entrance tickets and going into the park Simon turned to the children.

"If you two want to go off and ride the rides on your own you can, I think we will all meet up for lunch at the Ghostly Rib Shack around 12.00 noon " he said to them.

"Ok then dad see you later" they ran off in the direction of the rides.

Simon and Joanne headed towards the haunted garden where hands came out of the ground and the headstones sung songs and danced around. At 11.45 Joanne and Simon made their way towards the Restaurant. They found a table and ordered something to drink while they waited for the kids to arrive. 12.00 came and went, No Kids, 12.30 came and went, still no kids and by this time they were getting very worried.

"I think we should go and see security" said Joanne to her husband in a slightly shaky voice.

"Yes" he replied "I think that is a good idea"

They asked the waitress where the would find the security desk and she said

"Go to the park entrance and just before you get to the gates you will see what looks like a cave. Go in there and ask for Ted Layman he will help you."

Ted layman was having a really boring day. Nothing had happed that day and all he was doing was sitting at his desk reading the paper with his feet up sipping steaming hot coffee. Although he was bored out of his skin he loved his job at Spooky Hollow. He enjoyed being in charge of the large group of people that worked at the park, but what he didn't realize was that today was going to be the start of something that would give him more things to do than he ever thought he would be able to handle.

The door to Ted's Air-conditioned cave opened and in came Mr. and Mrs. Peabody.

"Erm excuse me" Joanne said to the plump security guard sitting behind the desk reading the paper, "could we speak to Ted Layman please?"

"Yes mam I'm Ted what can I do for you?" he asked.

"Our two children were supposed to meet us for lunch at 12.00 and they didn't turn up"

"I shouldn't worry, they have probably forgotten the time but I will get a description and announce it over the PA" he said

He collected the description of what they were wearing and then announced it to the park.

"Ladies and Gentlemen may I have you attention please. There are two children missing one is called TJ she is 13 and is wearing a blue roll neck top and green pants. Luke who is 15 is wearing a Hummer T-Shirt and Blue jeans with cowboy boots. If you see either of these two children please ask them to report to the security hut near the exit. Thank you and enjoy your day at Spooky Hollow."

"I'm afraid all we can do now is wait, but please don't worry. They have probably met up with some friends and have just forgotten" He said "if they re not back by 3.00 we will have to telephone the police"

"There was an argument last week." Simon told the security guard. "Luke and TJ had been round a friend's house and they said they were going to be home at 4.00 they didn't get home till 10.00 and we came down on them hard. That's why we are here today to make it up to them. They threatened to run away and maybe they have."

"Right." He said "I am going to phone the police because if they have run away then they need to know so that they can be on the look out for them." He got straight onto the phone and dialled his friend at the local police station.

He told them exactly what had happened and that they should send a unit to Spooky Hollow. He also said that the whole town should be alerted of the situation and that they should be on the look out.

It had been 5 hours since the Peabodys had told Ted about TJ and Luke going missing and they still hadn't turned up.

"Oh Simon I don't know what I would do if anything has happened to them" Joanne said as they sipped hot coffee.

"Don't worry Joanne they have probably got lost somewhere in the park. They will find them I promise."

The 5 police officers that had been searching the park came back and told Ted that a person had informed him that she saw two teenagers fitting the description of TJ and Luke queuing for the Ghost train ride and that she was on the same train as them but she didn't see them get off.

"Did she say where they were sitting in the train?" Ted asked the tall burley police officer.

"Yes" he replied "she said that they were sitting in the back of the train. She was two carts in front of them. We have conducted a search of the ride and the mine tunnels and there is no evidence that anybody has been down there since the park was opened 2 weeks ago."

Ted turned to Mr. and Mrs. Peabody and said "I'm afraid there is nothing we can do now. We have informed the town of the disappearances and we have men searching for them but there is no point of you staying here."

"Thank you officer." Simon said with tears in his eyes.

They got up and left the park by the same entrance that they came in both thinking about the children's happy faces when they had entered earlier that day.

# Chapter Seven

# The Haunt-INN Hotel and the Peabodys

The press either had not found out about the disappearances of TJ and Luke or someone was paying them to keep quite, as nothing had been published.

Business was booming at Spooky Hollow and at Doxam International but the customers felt that there was something missing. The customer comment cards revealed exactly what they thought was missing. Maddox Lewis was constantly reading the comment cards and making changes and adaptations to the park so that people would know that their comments weren't going unnoticed. It was Monday morning while Maddox was sitting at home reading the paper that he got a call from the head of customer services at Spooky Hollow, Robert Nicholls.

"I'm sorry to disturb you while you are relaxing" said Robert. He was a tall man with silvery gray hair and a kind nature. "But this weeks customer comment cards are all saying that there should be a hotel owned by Spooky Hollow. I didn't know what you wanted me to do about it."

"Well they will get a surprise very soon" aforementioned Maddox "thank you for calling Robert." He put down the phone just as Suzy came in.

"Who was that honeybunch?" she asked, putting down a fresh cup of tea for Maddox.

"Robert from Spooky Hollow. He was telling me that the families visiting Spooky Hollow want a hotel." He said grinning.

"They won't have to wait long then will they" she replied also grinning.

"Well now seems a good a time as any to make the announcement I have been sitting on for some time. I'll see you later" and with that he kissed his wife good bye and left the house.

He got into his car and speed down I-4 towards his theme park.

Maddox walked through the gates and headed toward the Spooky Hollow Haunted T.V Network Studio.

SHHTVN was Spooky Hollows own T.V broadcasting center. It broadcasted Movies, cartoons and Spooky Hollows news. The Movies and Cartoons were all Spooky orientated and the cartoons were designed and produced by Spooky Studios. SHHTVN had only been going one week but it had already been a major hit and had also drawn a lot more business to the park. SHHTVN was broadcasted all over America and as Maddox walked into the studio all the employees cheered and one of them said,

"Better behave now that the boss is here." Maddox laughed and took out the speech from his pocket that he had written 3 days previously.

The studio crew prepared Maddox for his appearance on TV. The film crew said he had one minute before the cartoon Spooky Spooky Creepy Creepy was interrupted for his special report. Maddox situated himself behind the reporter's desk and started to fiddle with his tie. Fiddling with his tie was something that Maddox did when he was nervous. He had on a black suit with a purple and black tie.

"5,4,3,2"

"Ladies and Gentleman Boys and Girls of all ages." Maddox said. "Since Spooky Hollow opened 4 weeks ago I have been dying to make this little announcement, and now that a lot of people have been filling out comment cards saying that they travelled on Doxam International, travelled in Spooky limousines and spent time in Spooky Hollow. The customers think that there should be a hotel owned by Spooky Hollow. Well I have great pleasure and pride in announcing that in two days time Spooky Hollow will be opening a hotel in the theme parks vicinity. The hotel would have been opened the same time as the theme park but we have had delays. Guests will enjoy a haunted experience with noises, lights and spooky spirits. Thank you for watching and have a good night."

Joanne Peabody turned off the T.V after hearing Maddox's speech. It had been two weeks since Joanne and Simon had seen their children, and now they had resigned themselves to the fact that they were never going to see them again. They had done everything in their power to find them. They had even gone on SHHTVN and asked for anybody with information to come forward. Nobody so far had done so. Simon and Joanne still felt they had not done enough.

Joanne had phoned Luke's cell phone a couple of days after their disappearances but she only got Ted Layman in the security hut.

"Hello" said Ted

"Luke is that you?"

"No this is Ted Layman at Spooky Hollow. We had this phone turned in yesterday. The lady said she found it in a bush when she picked up a piece of trash that had fallen out of the trash can."

Joanne put the phone down and then burst into one of her uncontrollable crying spurts.

As Joanne thought about her missing children the more she blamed herself

"If only I hadn't been so mean to them the night they were late home" she moaned at her husband one night over dinner.

"It's not your fault" he replied "its mine I shouldn't have let them go in the first place." Each other blamed themselves for the runaway and they came no closer to finding their beloved children.

Maddox left SHHTVN and got into his car. He travelled back up I-4 to his house. While driving he was thinking about the new security systems that he had had installed almost two weeks ago. The security systems were activated by an ID card with a barcode on it that was issued to you when you entered the park. The badges had a picture of the holder, the date and your own personal identification number. The cards were scanned by electronic readers which were linked to the Spooky Hollows main frame computer system. The readers were situated at ride entrances and ride exits. They helped Maddox and the staff at Spooky Hollow keep a track of park attendance and if anybody in the park was lost any employee could go into the main computer system and track a person with his or her name or his or her ID number. The computer will tell the viewer how long a person was on a ride for and how long they were in the park. Maddox's intention was to install a system like this for security reasons but the date was brought forward by the disappearances of the two children. Maddox knew what it was like to loose a loved one and he didn't want anybody else going through what the Peabodys did. At least with the new systems the police would be able to get a rough idea where they had gone in the time frame of leaving the park.

"Why the sad face darling" Suzy asked her husband when he got home.

"I've been trying to think of ways to improve the security systems" he replied.

Suzy remembered back to the day when the men had come to fit the readers.

"Did you hear about those two kids disappearing?" the computer technician said.

"Yeah I did. They said they ran away but I think it has something to do with this park" Rupert the supervisor replied.

Suzy was sitting in her office cubical three sections away from where the men were talking but she could hear every word they said. She had already cried her eyes out the night before about the children and she could feel the tears welling up in her eyes again. She tried to control herself but she couldn't. Then without warning, she burst into tears. Her friend Amy came over to console her but she was distraught.

"No parent should have to go through loosing their children." She sobbed through her gushing tears.

The memory was still fresh in Suzy's mind and even the thought of it now made tears come to her eyes.

"I couldn't bare it if we lost one of our children" she said. Hugging her husband.

As the billionaire had promised, the Haunt-Inn Hotel was open two days after his speech.

Maddox and his family gathered out side the hotel's new entrance. The excited crowd waited for him to give his speech and for the hotel to be officially opened. Maddox turned on the microphone that was fitted to the podium and said the commonly known testing words. The crowd fell silent.

"Ladies and gentlemen boys and girls of all ages. I want to thank all of you for coming to the opening of the Haunt- Inn Hotel. The opening marks the last phase in my dream. My dream was to have a Theme park where families can come and enjoy themselves in a safe environment. To have an airline so that families can travel in style and fun and to have a hotel, so at the end of a hard theme parking day you can go and lay your heads down. My dream is now complete. Well at least until I come up with another one" the crowd laughed. "Anyway I hope you all enjoy the new addition to Spooky Hollow. I am sorry it wasn't ready to be opened when the park was but we have had technical difficulties. Ladies and gentlemen I give you the third and final phase The Haunt-Inn Hotel." Maddox cut the ribbon. The crowd whistled and cheered. Spooky Hollow was now complete.

# Chapter Eight

## Two more disappearances

Vicky, Phillipa, Carl and Craven decided that they would have a day out at Spooky Hollow. Vicky had wanted to go ever since the park opened but they hadn't had the time, but now the four friends were piled into Phillipa's blue Mitsubishi Spyder. Phillipa had gotten up at 7.00 am that morning and had taken a shower then gone to pick up Vicky, from there they picked up Craven and Carl. The drive down to Spooky Hollow was rather boring but they managed to pass the time by playing number games and listening to music.

When they arrived at Spooky Hollow the guard in the gate booth gave them a ticket which had the number of the parking space that was free. This had been Suzy's idea as she was always moaning about the parking when they went to theme parks. The guard took the make, model and licence plate number of Phillipa's car. They drove to their allotted parking space but it took them 10 minutes longer as Phillipa took a wrong turn and ended up having to go out of the park and come back in again. They bought their tickets for the park admission and were issued with their new ID cards. The four friends walked through the main gate and Vicky's jaw dropped. She was in theme park heaven. Phillipa and Vicky were best friends and went everywhere together. Vicky was tall with blonde hair. She was the best looking one of the two. Phillipa was short with brown hair. Carl and Craven looked identical even though they weren't even related. Both were 5ft 11in and both had ginger hair. They were a real pair of practical jokers. Once when they were at the beach, they found a crab, Carl captured it and put it down Phillipa's bathing suit. She screamed and when she found out who had done it she didn't speak to him for a whole week.

The four decided they would go to the haunted nature experience first which was like a safari but with animal skeletons running around. Vicky's favourite was the ghost birds. They flew above their heads squawking and chirping. All four of them were amazed at the amount of technology that was in the park. Following an escapade in the haunted Amazon the team went to the haunted graveyard. Vicky got a shock when what she thought was a statue grabbed her from behind. She screamed and made everyone turn to look at her. After her experience with the "lively" statue Vicky suggested that they go and get something to eat, so they headed towards the spooky rib shack to satisfy the hunger growing in their stomachs.

After the very filling delicious lunch Vicky, Phillipa, Craven and Carl decide to go on the tour that was being offered at the Haunt-Inn hotel, as they didn't think that they should go straight on a roller coaster after lunch. Upon heading to the hotel Phillipa was frightened by a mechanical trash can that yelled insults at everyone that tried to put any thrash into it.

"Find a bin that cares." It said when Phillipa tried to put her gum wrapper in it.

After about 30 minutes of listening to a guy prattling on about how the hotel was fitted with water beds, had state of the art security systems and the fact that SHHTVN was linked to all of the hotel room televisions and there were interactive demos of the park, the four were getting bored. They broke off from the group just before heading into the ballroom.

"Man, he droned on so much he may have well been a ghost himself." Said Craven. They laughed until a receptionist that was passing them said

"He sounded like that because he is computerized. He is basically a hologram"

The wind was knocked out of Craven at this comment. The receptionist walked away back to her desk.

They decided they would go and walk round the haunted safari so they made there way to the enclosed building that stood a little of the pathway to the left of the Haunt-Inn hotel. One of the park engineers who was working on fixing the skeleton tiger told the four friends how everything in the park was computerized. When he told them how much the technology in the park had cost Carl yelled out.

"$150,000,000" he gasped

"Yes" replied the engineer "and that's not including the Haunt-Inn Hotel"

The amazed four walked away

"I want to go on the Haunted ghost train ride. Anybody else want to join me?" asked Vicky the other three were up for it so they made their way to the ride entrance. It took them about an hour to queue as it was the most popular ride in the park. Round and round they went queue after queue, but eventually it evened out and they could see the little brown mine carts that were used for the train. Upon having their barcode cards scanned for about the 7th time that day Vicky said

"Why do we have to keep having these damn cards scanned?"

"To keep you safe" said the ride manager. "how many?"

"4" said Craven.

"All of the 4 seater carts are full, you can either wait for the next train or there are two, two seater carts at the back.

They decided that they would take the carts as they had been waiting in line for an hour or so and now they were actually at the platform they didn't want to wait any longer. Vicky and Phillipa fought over who was going to sit in the back. Phillipa won and sat in the back with Craven.

The lap bar closed and they set off bumping down the little tracks. The cart went through the mining village and amongst the ghostly ghastly noises they could hear a little girl in the front of the train screaming at the top of her lungs. She evidently didn't like ghosts. Phillipa was laughing until a ghost flew in front of her and she screamed. The carts trundled up a dark incline and stopped for about 2 seconds. (Which was just enough time to panic) then plunged the 100ft drop into the mine. Phillipa was screaming the whole way. Then the screaming stopped and, they pulled into the station and Vicky looked round to talk to her two friends, but neither were there

"Where'd they go?" she said. The lap bar lifted and they got out of the cart. There was no sign of Phillipa or Craven anywhere. Vicky and Carl went outside and waited by the exit in case Phillipa and Craven had managed to get out before them although Vicky didn't see how that was possible because the lap bar hadn't even gone up when she had looked around. Vicky took out her cell phone and tried to call Phillipa. She dialled the number but the metal Mickey voice on the other end said.

"Please hold your call is being transferred to an automated voice mail system."

They waited for another 10 minutes watching the people coming off the ride chatting about it and discussing their favourite parts. The 10 minutes came and went and Phillipa and Craven still hadn't turned up. Vicky and Carl were now getting worried so they headed to the security hut to report them missing.

Yet again Ted was having a boring day. He was thinking about changing jobs. Although the pay was good and he liked being in charge he just didn't get to do as much as he liked.

The doors to the hut opened and in came Vicky and Carl. Ted hastily shoved the donut he was eating into his desk draw and quickly swallowed the piece that he had already bitten off

"What can I do for you" Ted asked them politely.

"Our friends have gone missing and we would like to know if you can help us." Replied Carl.

"When did you last see them" asked Ted as he pulled a notepad from the same drawer that had his concealed donut in. the donut has leaked jam onto the pad but Ted wiped it off with a tissue and took out a pen from the yellow and green pot on his desk.

"The last time that we saw them was when we got onto the Haunted Ghost train ride." Said Vicky, now recovering from the shock of how disorganized Ted was. Ted jotted down the information then said

"Names?"

"Phillipa and Craven."

He dialled 2,9,6,4 on his desk phone.

"Phillipa and Craven please report the security hut Phillipa and Craven please report to the security hut. Thank you and enjoy your day at Spooky Hollow.

"We have to wait ten minutes until we can access the barcode scanners." Ted informed the worried friends. The ten minutes came and went and still there was no sign of Phillipa and Craven.

"Ok" said Ted "what are their last names?"

"Phillipa Mayes and Craven Gray."

Ted typed in the names and up popped Phillipa and Craven's Log file.

"The log said they got on the ride at 3:15.03 and got off at 3:21.09"

Ted brought up Vicky and Carl's log files to compare them.

"It says you got on the ride at 3:15.03 and got off at 3:21.15."

They checked out before us?" Vicky said.

Ted asked for the make and model of Phillipa's car. Vicky told him and he pulled up the parking log inventory. There were three Mitsubishi Spyders in the lot. One blue one green and one red. Phillipa's car was still there.

"The car park exit scanner says they checked out at 3.35. Which was 5 minutes ago" Ted said looking at the clock on the wall. "I'm calling the police."

# Chapter Nine

## The investigation

The police arrived after closing and conducted a thorough search of the park.

"I am going to call Phillipa and Cravens parents to see if they have gone home" said Detective Julie Garrett to her husband Sam who was chief of detectives. Julie Garrett was 5ft 6in with blonde hair, which was always tied back in a bun at the back of her head. She didn't let anything ever get in the way of her career. Sam was 5ft 11in with brown spiky hair.

She got the numbers from Vicky and placed the calls.

"Hello" said Phillipa's mum.

"Mrs. Mayes has your daughter come home from Spooky Hollow, as her car is here but she and her friend Craven checked out of the park at 3.50."

"No she hasn't come home" replied Mrs. Mayes, now sounding rather worried.

"You and your husband had better come to the park." The detective informed her

"We will be there right away" said the worried parent.

Julie called Cravens parents but had the same response from them. She had asked them to come to the park. Detective Garrett interviewed Vicky and Carl about the last time they saw their friends. She asked for very specific details so that she could gather as much information as she could. After the interview was completed she sent three officers to the Ghost Train ride to see if they could find out anything else.

"They've probably just run off" said officer 1752 as they walked down the narrow path to the ride.

"Yeh that's what I think but I also think that there is something spooky about this."

He looked at his fellow colleagues who were both laughing at him.

"What's so funny?" he asked

"You said there was something spooky about the disappearances. We are in a spooky orientated theme park."

"Oh that." He said sniggering.

They carried on walking towards the ride. When they finally arrived they walked down the queue line without having to wait.

"I wish it could be like this when the park's open" said Officer 1752, smiling.

"Me too" piped up Officer Brooker. "I hate queuing. All of the rides at Spooky Hollow had to be run twelve times after the park had closed.

They also had to be scanned by computer to make sure that the track was all in order and that there were no brakes or cracks. When the three officers got to the ride platform the manager told them they would have to wait five minutes for the scanner to finish before they could perform their investigation. The officers stood waiting impatiently at the end of the line while the computer finished its scan. After what seemed like ages, although it was only four minutes, the ride manager called them over and gave them instructions on where the stairs and railings were so that they didn't fall down any of the mine shafts. Officer 142 Webster hopped down onto the track and pulled out his torch. Officer 192 Robson and officer 1752 Nicholls followed suit. The three walked down the narrow track and into the dark mining town. It was cold and damp, officer Nichols could feel the hairs on the back of her neck standing up, however she wasn't going to admit to them that she was scared. The town was so realistic and moving, that if they hadn't have known better they would have thought that they had stepped back in time. They searched every one of the sets. They searched every nook, every cranny but they didn't find a scrap of evidence.

"I think we had better call Maddox Lewis." Said Chief Detective Sam Garrett.

Ted looked up Maddox's cell phone number which was in the black Rolodex on his desk.

"Maddox this is Ted Layman at Spooky Hollow speaking."

"Hello what can I do for you Ted?" Maddox asked

"Well, this is kind of a difficult think to say but erm, two people have disappeared and the police think that they went missing in the park although the scanners say they checked out."

"I'll be there straight away." Replied Maddox. They both hung up and Detective Julie Garrett made her way over to Mr. and Mrs. Mayes, and Mr. and Mrs. Gray to inform them of the outcome of the search.

"We have searched the ghost train ride and in fact the whole park. We have found no evidence that Phillipa and Craven have been here. The only reason we know they have been here is that her car is in the car park and her two friends were with them. We have called the owner of the park Maddox Lewis and he is going to come into the park and present a special report on SHHTVN."

Craven's mum had tears forming in her eyes and Phillipa's mum was already crying deep, heart wrenching sobs.

"Why.........would.......she.......run.......away?" she hiccupped.

"It's all your stupid sons fault" she yelled tearing away from her husband who was trying to console her and keep control of his emotions at the same time. "And now I bet he has run off with her against her will." She continued to shout at Mrs. Gray. She ran towards her and Mrs. Gray had to jump out of the way as Caroline Mayes dived at her. Ted jumped out from behind his desk to separate the fighting parents. This was a remarkable feat as Ted was about 250lbs and couldn't secure a paper bag let alone separate a pair of emotional parents. After Caroline and Beatrice had been separated Maddox came through the door. The sight that greeted him was not a pretty one. Tom Mayes had hold of his wife struggling with the emotional women who was trying to resume her fighting with Beatrice.

Detective Julie Garrett had Chris Gray in a head lock and Ted had Beatrice pinned to the wall.

"It's all your fault." Yelled Caroline. "It's all your fault" she begun again but Maddox cut in.

"WHAT ON EARTH IS GOING ON?" he said. But he already knew the answer. Ted gasped an explanation. He was gasping because he was still trying to retain the emotional Mrs. Gray. Maddox asked Mr. and Mrs. Mayes to follow him. They followed him outside however they were reluctant. He led them out of the security hut and down the little narrow path to his wife's office. Tom told Maddox their theory of what had happened and Maddox said

"Yes that's what I think has happened but at the moment we can't be sure." They went through a set of double doors into the air conditioned office block. They followed Maddox into his wife's little cubicle and he introduced them.

Suzy was very upset to here about the loss of their daughter. Maddox was hoping to get off to the SHHTVN studio straight away but he had to stay for a further 5 minutes and comfort his crying wife when he had her under control he slipped out of the cubical and headed toward the studio thinking of what he was going to say. The studio crew greeted him with sombre looks on their faces. Clearly they had heard the news also. They prepared him for the camera and as he seated himself behind the news desk one of the cameramen began the count down to when Maddox would be on-air.

"5...4...3...2..."

"Ladies and Gentlemen. I have a very important message for you all. There are two people missing one of them is called Phillipa Mayes who is 5ft 5in tall with shoulder length dark brown hair. The name of the second person is Craven Gray who is 6ft with short ginger hair. They were last seen in Spooky Hollow but we have reason to believe that they left the park. Please be on the look out for these children. The local police have a reward for any valid information leading to their safe return. If you have any information please call 555-089-5781. Thank You had have a good evening"

"Cut"

Phillipa and Cravens Parents went back to their homes, after making statements there was nothing else they could do that evening.

That afternoon when Simon Peabody got home from work his wife told him about Maddox's report on SHHTVN.

"There's something about that park" she said "It's not the kids running away it's the park, I find it very weird that four people have now disappeared and not a scrap of evidence has been found to suggest that they have disappeared."

Simon looked at his wife and nodded. It was all he could do, he felt so miserable.

After his report, Maddox went to see his wife to exchange keys.

"Christina is going to pick the kids up from soccer practice." Maddox said to his wife, who was still very shock up about the disappearances. "So I am going to leave you my car and I'm going to take your SUV so that I can give Vicky and Carl a lift home."

"Ok" she said very subdued.

Maddox put the keys to his Ferrari on her desk. Unbeknown to him that it would be the last time he drove his red sports car for a long while. He took the Hummer keys out of her hand bag and left the accounts building.

"Mr. Lewis" said Vicky "what do you think happened to our friends?"

"I don't know" said Maddox "But I'm certainly going to find out"

The rest of the 45 minute drive was very uneventful unless you include the time when an idiotic teenager in a customized Honda Civic pulled in front of Maddox Causing him to slam on the brakes.

He swore very loudly and flicked the driver off who responded with the same signal.

"And these are the future of our society. It doesn't inspire much confidence in the younger race." He said to himself more than Vicky and Carl.

After dropping the two kids at their houses which were both located in Winter Springs, Maddox headed straight for his brothers house. After going past the 70 mph speed limit by 30 mph Maddox decided he had better slow down. He didn't really think his brother had anything to so with the disappearances but in today's society you never know. He definitely had a motive but did he have the guts?

# Chapter Ten

## The Cruise and the Concrete Barrier

Maddox pulled up to his brother's house and sat there for a while. Trying to decide whether or not to speak to him about the unusual disappearances. He decided he would because he knew that from the beginning he had been against the idea of Maddox getting his father's inheritance. After all he designed the park; in fact Ronald probably knew more about Spooky Hollow than Maddox did. He got out of his wife's Hummer and walked down his brother's pathway towards the big oak front door. With the money Ronald had received from Maddox for the designing of the theme park rides he had brought himself a new car and had renovated the inside and outside of his house. He had also had a pool built. Ronald's new Maserati was parked on the driveway glinting in the evening setting sun. The sky was a purpley pink color when Maddox rung the door bell. He waited for a couple of minutes before walking around to the screen porch. He saw his brother in the swimming pool so he opened the screen door and went inside.

"Hey Maddy" Ronald said. (Maddy was Maddox's nickname that he had had since he was about 5)

"Ronald. I have something to ask you about Spooky Hollow and it's not going to be an easy question to ask." Maddox stuttered then said "do you know anything about the disappearances?"

"Of course I don't." he replied sharply. Maddox was suppressed by the sudden reply and it disturbed him slightly. "How could you suspect me?" he asked.

"I don't suspect you" Maddox replied "I just wondered if you knew anything that was all."

"Well I'm glad that you are here anyway as I have something to tell you" said Ronald.

Maddox listened intensively hoping against hope that it would be something about the disappearances, but it wasn't.

"Debbie and I are going on a cruise we are leaving tomorrow."

"Oh right." said Maddox. He didn't know what to say. It striked him odd that the day that two people disappear at Spooky Hollow, Ronald decides to go on a cruise.

"Is this a recent decision or had it been booked for a while?" Maddox asked his brother when he surfaced from a dive.

"We booked it this afternoon, we need a brake."

Maddox left the pool screen without even saying goodbye, he got into the hummer and drove off. His mind was thinking about what Ronald had said. As he went pass the Deland Deltona sign on I-4 he said to himself "He designed the rides he could have quite easily have built in a way to kidnap people without anybody knowing." Maddox was so deep in thought he didn't know what was happening until it was too late. He slammed on the brakes but not soon enough. He hit a concrete barrier, ricocheted off and spun into the retaining wall. Maddox felt the SUV crumble in around him. He remembered no more.

The main doors to Deland hospital slid open and Suzy, Paul and Misty walked in. Suzy had red blood shot eyes and Misty and Paul were crying. Suzy walked up to the clerk at the main desk, her high heels clicking on the polished marble floor.

"Could you please tell me what room Maddox Lewis is in" she sniffed. The receptionist looked at the computer screen then when she found what she was looking for she said

"He's in room 7-014"

Suzy and her two children ran to the long list next to the elevator that displayed the room numbers and the floors that they were located on. They found the room number they were looking for so Suzy turned to the children and said

"Kids go and sit in the waiting room until I send for you." Suzy didn't know what kind of state she would find her husband in. The two children did not go quietly.

"If you two do not go and sit down you will be grounded for a year." She yelled. A few people that were about to get out the elevator closed the doors and rose to the next floor to save walking by the enraged female. Suzy called the elevator back down to the first floor and got in. She pressed the button for the 3rd floor and as the doors closed she tried not to think about what kind of condition her adorable husband would be in. There was only two other people in the elevator. An elderly man and a disabled woman which could only be his wife. The elevator stopped at the 2nd floor and the two exited. The doors closed and the elevator ground back into life, the electrical humming ringing in Suzy's ears. The doors opened at the 3rd floor and Suzy exited. The walk down to room 7-014 seemed to be one of the longest Suzy had ever walked. Upon turning the corner she saw the room number that she was looking for. She went up to the door and peeked through the window. She couldn't see her husband as the nurse was bending over the bed. The only thing that she could see was his bandaged foot protruding out from under the sheets. As the nurse moved out of the way Suzy caught a glimpse of her husband and gasped. Maddox's hands and feet were bound tightly with bandages; his face was cut above his eye which was probably caused by glass. The heart monitor was beeping normally. Suzy hesitated before putting her hand on the door handle and turning it. The door creaked open and the nurse turned around to look at the person entering. Suzy walked up to the nurse and said

"How's he doing? I'm his wife"

"He's not too bad" she replied "the truck took the brunt of it, he has a broken wrist but he will heal up nicely" The nurse tuned to leave.

"Nurse" Suzy said "There are two children in the waiting room on the first floor; you do think that you could bring them up?" The nurse nodded and left pulling the door shut behind her. Suzy sat down in the old creaky chair that was next to the bed. Maddox stirred.

"What happened?" Suzy whispered to him. Very sleepily Maddox replied

"I suspected that the disappearances at Spooky Hollow had something to do with Ronald, so I went to his house to talk to him about it. He told me that he and Debbie were going on a cruise. I thought this was a bit weird as Ronald gets sea sick very easily." Maddox paused for a minute trying to remember what had happened. "Then I was driving home when I hit piece of tire that I think had been shed off a truck, I lost control and then" he paused again. "I don't remember what happened. I guess the truck took the brunt of it. I'm sorry Suzy I know how much you loved your SUV."

"Oh don't be stupid Maddox the point is your alive and in somewhat good shape." Replied Suzy.

"The doctor said that I should be able to come home in about a week."

The door opened and in came misty and Paul.

"Daddy" Misty yelled. The little girl ran across the room and flung herself at her father. Maddox winced as her elbow hit his broken wrist. Paul walked casually over to his father trying his hardest to act like what he thought a mature teenager would in a circumstance like this. He failed miserably and also flung himself at his father but being careful not to land on anything broken. Suzy turned and left the room due to the tears that were pouring down her face. Maddox saw her leave but didn't call her back or ask where she was going as he knew that the whole ordeal had been stressful on her as well as the children. When Suzy had finished crying she went back into the room where her husband was lying. He looked very uncomfortable due to the combined weight of both his children but Maddox being Maddox didn't say anything.

"I'm going to call your Brother and Mother and tell them what has happened."

"No, Don't" Said Maddox. "Mother will only worry and I need Ronald to go on his cruise to see if my theory is correct."

"What do you mean?"

"Later" Maddox said as he saw Paul shift his head a little so that he could hear what they were saying.

Five days after the accident, Dr. Lipinski said that Maddox was on the mend and that he could go home.

Suzy arrived at the Hospital later that evening to pick him up. She was driving her clapped out blue Chevy Suburban.

"I thought you gave that to your friend Lauren when I brought you the Hummer." Said Maddox when he saw what his wife was driving.

"I did but I borrowed it back until we got a new car, because how was I going to take the kids to school in your car?"

"Strap one to the hood like a deer." Maddox suggested. They both burst out laughing. It had been a long time since they had laughed so hard.

Maddox wondered if his present for Suzy had been delivered yet. His hand moved to his pocket where the new set of keys were. They didn't talk much on the way home but Maddox did ask if there was any news on Phillipa and Craven.

"No dear there isn't, but I am sure the police are doing everything they can."

They pulled up to the driveway of their house but there was already a vehicle there.

"Who do we know that drives a Lincoln Navigator?" Suzy asked her husband.

"I don't know as we do know anybody that drives that type of car" said Maddox trying to fight down a laugh. Suzy got out of the truck and went round to the passenger side to help her husband. They walked up the drive toward the shiny black Navigator. Suzy let go of her husband and walked up to the front of the SUV where a big Bow was tied on to the Lincoln symbol. There was also an envelope stuck in the grill. Suzy shot her husband an inquiring look as if to say "You didn't." He didn't say anything. Suzy picked up the envelope and tore it open.

*My Darling wife Suzy,*

*I hope you like your new SUV as much as your last one. Sorry it took so long.*

*Love you lots,*

*Maddox*

*P.S It has the government's highest safety rating.*

Maddox tossed her the keys and she caught them with a soft jingle. She opened the Navigator.

"Cream Leather interior, 6CD Changer, Independent DVD players in the back. Heated and Air conditioned seats, Sun Roof, you name it it's got it." Maddox informed his wife.

"Thank you so much" Suzy said hugging her husband. She started the engine then said "you coming for a spin?"

"No thanks" he replied "I'm going to go and have a cup of coffee." He closed the door for his wife and walked off toward the house. Suzy screeched off up the road. It was quiet and cool inside the house, the children were still at a friends and the maid had left for the day.

Maddox padded in his bare feet across the hall way to the kitchen. Something about the park was niggling the back of his mind but he couldn't quite focus on it. Suzy had made a comment he couldn't quite remember, as he poured his coffee he only hoped that it would come back to him.

# Chapter Eleven

# Another visit from the abominable sister

Detectives Sam and Julie Garrett were having a really stressful day at the police station. The whole place was buzzing with people talking, phones ringing and computer keyboards groaning under the incessant typing of fingers. It was like the place had become a mad house since the disappearances of Phillipa and Craven. Sam was sitting in his office puzzling over the evidence they had which was nothing. Sam didn't know how somebody could kidnap (if that's actually what happened) four people without leaving one piece of evidence. He was still puzzling when his wife came in.

"I think we need to go and talk to Mr. Lewis about his theme park."

"That's what I came in here for; the boss is nagging at me to get this case solved and find those children."

"The thing that we need to establish is a motive. Why would he "kidnap" children in his own theme park? It's not the money. He has more than he can spend" said Sam

"I don't know, but if we go and see him maybe he will let something slip." Julie said as she got up from the seat that she was sitting on in front of her husband's desk.

If the detectives had gone to Maddox's office the day before they would have found it empty due to the fact that he was still at home recovering from his accident. Maddox had decided that he was bored of sitting at home just watching TV. So he packed his briefcase and called his friend Benny. Benny had been Maddox's friend since middle school. He also owned a chauffeuring company and would probably be quite happy to drive Maddox around.

"Good morning, you've reached Benny Matheson chauffeurs. How may I help you?" The receptionist asked.

"I would like to speak to Benny please" Maddox asked.

"One moment please"

Maddox heard music being played in the background. He hated being put on hold but he didn't have to wait long.

"Benny Matheson".

"Hey Benny it's Maddox how's it going?"

"Maddox, how are you? I heard about your accident. Are you alright?"

"Well I'm doing better now but I have a broken wrist so I can't drive which is why I'm calling you."

"Say no more, say no more. When and where do you want me to pick you up from?"

"Can you pick me up from my house in Spruce Creek and I need you to pick me up as soon as you can."

"I'll pick you up personally."

"Thanks Benny I knew I could count on you." Maddox put down the house phone and went to the kitchen where he could hear his Nextel beeping. He picked up his yellow and black phone (His children called it the Yellow Peril)

"Go ahead." He said to his wife.

"Maddox I have just got a call from Paul, he tells me that he has soccer practice tonight so I'm going to be home late as I have to pick up Misty from school and then go and get Paul, take him to practice and wait for them to finish then I'll get something to eat on the way home."

Maddox tried to reply but all he got was the annoying beeeeep that Nextel users hear so frequently. He swore very loudly. After about a minute of beeping and swearing Maddox managed to reply to his wife.

"Ok, I have called Benny" Suzy knew who Benny was as all three of them were in the same math class at school. "And he is going to pick me up and take me to the office as I am fed up of sitting at home on the sofa watching TV." Maddox released the hammer on the side of the phone and his wife immediately said

"Are you sure that your ready to go back to work."

"Suzy if I have to sit at home for one more day doing nothing I'll go stir crazy. I've already been here for two weeks."

"Ok well just be careful, speak to you later, love you, bye."

"Bye" he replied. He closed the top on his phone and went to the study where his briefcase was. Christina the maid came out of the bathroom.

"Christina I am going into the office so you can have the rest of the day off if you would like."

"Thank you Mr. Lewis."

Maddox picked up his briefcase and as he did the door bell rang. Maddox opened it and saw his old friend standing on the door step.

"You ready?" asked Benny

"That was fast I only called you ten minutes ago."

"Yeah I know but I had my secretary transfer all my phone calls to my cell phone. I was on my way back to the office when I got your call and I thought as I had the Limo I would pick you up in style." Maddox caught sight of the black Lincoln Town Car Limousine that was parked in the driveway behind Maddox's Ferrari.

Maddox closed the front door and followed Benny to the limo. He got into the back, the leather was hot from where the car had been sitting in the sun, but it soon cooled down when they set off towards the Champs building.

Maddox and Benny chatted about their business and what either of them would do if they became president. The whole talk was ludicrous but it helped to pass the time. After saying goodbye to his chauffeur, and old pal Maddox went off up to his office. His secretary was very surprised and happy to see him. She gave him the list of the messages and people that he had to call; she also gave him the stack of mail. He went into his office and seated himself behind his desk. It's nice to be back, He thought to himself.

Maddox was now having a good day. In one hour he had yelled at the manager of Spooky Hollow for not helping the police with the investigation of the missing people, He had fired three Spooky Hollow employees for stealing and he had brought two new planes for Doxam International. He was really happy until the doors to his office banged open and in strode Samantha.

"So you're still living then" she said with malice. "What a pity, after all there's still time. It's a shame really because I could have some of the Lewis money from your wife."

"You're bloody evil. Do you know that the way you treat people is atrocious and people like you don't deserve to live." Maddox yelled at her. "And how did you know that I was back at work" he asked in a slightly lower tone of voice. He didn't need to ask how she knew about the accident as it had been broadcast on Fox local news. There were also some rather disturbing pictures of him being cut out of the wreckage and carried of in an ambulance.

"I knew that you were back because I called your secretary and she told me that you were back, she didn't know it was me though. I can be very convincing when I want to."

Maddox didn't beat about the bush this time he just came out and said it

"I think that you have something to do with the disappearances at Spooky Hollow."

"HOW DARE YOU" she yelled at him "I may be a lot of things but I am not a killer."

"I didn't say they were dead" said Maddox, thinking to himself that he had finally made her drop herself in trouble.

"How dare you I'm leaving" Samantha was extremely angry, so much so that if she could breath fire Maddox's building would be ablaze. She turned on her heel and stormed out, pushing past Sam and Julie who were coming in through the main doors.

# Chapter Twelve

## The Investigation Continues

The Doors to Maddox's office opened again and in came Sam and Julie Garrett.

"Mr. Lewis we need to talk to you about the disappearances at your theme park. We think you may know something about it." said Sam

Maddox looked puzzled for a moment then said

"Ok but I'm not sure how much help I can be. I thought it had something to do with my brother so I went to his house to ask him about it. The reason that I suspected my brother was because he designed the rides and he could quite easily have built in some kidnapping device. Plus the fact that he still holds a grudge against me because I received our father's inheritance." Maddox paused for a few seconds and waited until Sam had finished writing on his notepad. "When

I went to his house he told me that he and his wife were going on a cruise. I was thinking about it when I had the accident.

"You said that you thought it was your brother. What changed your mind?" Julie said.

"Because my brother doesn't have the guts to kidnap children. My sister. Well there's another matter. She even came in to say that she wished I had died so that she could have got some of the Lewis money from my wife." Maddox paused again, took a sip of water from the glass on his desk and then said "I challenged her about the disappearances and she said she had nothing to do about it and stormed out. That was her, who was leaving as you came in.

"We'll need to speak to you brother and sister can we have a number to get hold of them?"

"Ronald has gone on a cruise and I don't have a contact number for him and I don't even know where Samantha is living let alone a number to call her so I am afraid I can't help you there." He replied.

"You're a rich man Mr. Lewis everybody knows that and if you are willing we can find out where she is living and even find out what her phone number is." said Julie

"I'm listening" Maddox replied.

"Well you can host a Grand Prize Draw where people can buy tickets and win a sum of money that you choose. People would be required to fill out a form. You just have to put a place on the form for an address and phone number" said Julie

"That's an excellent idea. I'll give a million dollars to the winner. That'll get her attention. I'll start the plans as soon as you leave." Maddox said to the police officers. He picked up one of his business cards of his desk, flipped it over to the blank backside and wrote his Nextel radio number on the back. He also wrote his cell phone number and his home number.

"If you need to get hold of me, call me on any of these numbers, if I'm not in you can leave a message with my wife." He passed the card to Julie who pocketed it. The two police officers got up, said good bye and left. When they were out of anybody's earshot Julie said.

"He's covering up for someone and I can't wait to find out who."

# Chapter Thirteen

## Something Odd and disturbing

Maddox began the preparations for the prize draw as soon as Sam and Julie left. First he called his secretary to tell her what he was going to do. Then he called his advertising agent, Sean. Sean had designed the original bill boards for Spooky Hollow.

"Hello" said Sean, when he answered the phone.

"Hey Sean, long time no speak" replied Maddox."

"Hey Maddox how you doing? I heard about your accident."

"I'm doing ok. The reason that I'm calling you is because I need you to do me a favour."

"Ok, but it depends what is it,"

Maddox told Sean about the Grand Prize Draw and what he wanted on the adverts.

"No probs. I'll have them done by this afternoon and I'll have the crew put them up in this evening."

"Thanks Sean I owe you one."

"Bye"

Maddox had ordered four billboard adverts and 30 posters. Maddox paged his secretary.

"Lisa could you get Detective Julie Garrett on the phone for me?"

"Certainly" she replied.

Maddox didn't have to wait long. Beep went the intercom to signal that there was an open line.

"Detective" asked Maddox.

"Yes Mr. Lewis what can I do for you?"

"I just wanted to let you know that I have set the wheels in motion for the Grand Prize Draw."

"That was quick; we only left your office 30 minutes ago."

"Well I don't hang about; anyway I have ordered 4 billboards and 30 posters. I am also going to go to Spooky Hollow and make an announcement on SHHTVN."

"Ok great, we are going to run a check on your sister can you tell us what her full name is, her birthday and her Social Security Number?"

"Samantha Jane Lewis." replied Maddox. "and her birthday is June 8th 1975. I don't know what her Social Security Number is, Sorry" They said goodbye and Maddox beeped Lisa.

"Lisa could you call Benny and ask him if he would come and collect me as we have to go down to Spooky Hollow."

"Ok Sir, will do"

Maddox did some paper work and was just about to call the manager of Doxam International when Lisa beeped his intercom,

"Maddox, Benny is here shall I send him in?"

"Yes please."

Maddox got up and turned off his desk lamp which he had had to turn on earlier in the day due to the fact that the sunshine had changed to a thunderstorm. As he picked up his brief case the office door opened and in came Benny.

"You ready?"

"Yup let's go."

"Where are we going?" Benny asked

"To Spooky Hollow to make a report on SHHTVN to trap my sister"

"What?"

"Oh you don't know do you ok let's get going and then I'll fill you in."

Maddox and Benny left the office and got into the elevator. This was one of the noisiest in the building.

"I really must get this damn thing fixed." Maddox said to himself more than to Benny.

Maddox asked Janet, the main receptionist if he could have two umbrellas. She produced a black and green spotted one and a black and white striped one. Maddox gave Benny the black and green spotted one.

"Thanks" he said sarcastically. The two approached the big glass doors which at this moment led out into what looked like a waterfall. Benny pushed open the doors and they made their way as fast as they could to the limo.

"I brought the excursion limo" said Benny "I thought that it would be safer in the rain than the Lincoln."

They got into the car, Maddox got into the front this time as he didn't feel like being cooped up in the back with hardly any light. They set off down I-4 to Kissimmee. The drive was very quite as neither of them were talking. Maddox did however tell Benny why he was having the Grand Prize Draw. Maddox suddenly thought of something and swore. He plucked his phone out of his left inside jacket pocket and dialled his office number.

"Maddox Lewis Industries" Lisa said.

"Lisa it's me I need you to do me a big favour. Can you go onto my computer and on the Z drive you will find the tickets and forms for the Grand Prize Draw. Can you print a copy off and fax it to Sean. Then can you call him, the number is in the rolodex on my desk, and ask him to print 10,000 copies then can you ask him if he would put that there will be a limit of 10,000 tickets sold."

"Ok will do" Said Lisa as she wrote down what Maddox told her. "I'm going to buy you an organizer for Christmas so that you don't forget anything else."

"Ha Ha Ha, Lisa I have to go I have a call coming in."

"Bye" she said

Maddox terminated the call to his secretary and answered the call that was waiting which turned out to be Detective Julie Garrett

"Mr. Lewis I have some news for you on your sister. We did a background check on her. She was arrested in 1995 for drug possession. She also took a computer programming course for four years. She then went to work for a computer company called Time Warp Computers" Maddox Gulped, "She quit last week and due to company policy her records were deleted from the computer system so we have still have no idea where she is."

"Got to go, call later" Maddox terminated the call and said "Step on it Benny we have to get to Spooky Hollow fast."

"Why what's the matter" asked Benny.

"That was the detective working on the disappearances at Spooky Hollow she told me that Samantha worked at Time Warp Computers."

"What's wrong with that?"

"Time Warp Computers is the computer company that designed and assembled the computers for Spooky Hollow. They were also the ones that designed the barcode scanners."

"Uh oh, not good" replied Benny.

Maddox didn't say anything for the rest of the journey. He hoped against hope that his sister hadn't worked on the computers but the way his luck had been going lately it was more than likely that she had.

# Chapter Fourteen

## The Computer

Benny slammed on the brakes outside the staff entrance to Spooky Hollow. Maddox jumped out the vehicle and ran as fast as he could to the control room. Every part of electrical equipment, every light and every air conditioner in the whole park and hotel could be controlled from this room. Maddox inserted his security card into the slot at the side of the solid glass door, which elevated to allow access to the restricted room. Maddox went into the room and sat down at the vacant seat in front of the second computer. All the computers in Spooky Hollow were linked to these two super computers that were contained in the control room. Oliver Taylor the chief technician at Spooky Hollow was sitting in front of the first computer, pounding the keys on the keyboard. He was so involved in what he was doing he didn't realize Maddox and Benny had entered.

"Hello Maddox" he said when he finally realized that they were there. Maddox grunted and Oliver, taking the hint resumed his incessant typing. The sound of plastic keys tapping was audible again. Maddox entered his user name (Maddy) and his password (Fuzzy) and hit enter.

Welcome to Spooky Hollow's main frame computer system, was displayed on the screen. Access to the main frame could be gained by any computer in Spooky hollow or at Maddox's office block, but only those with special usernames and passwords could gain access. There were only four people that had that capability and those four people were, Maddox, Suzy, Oliver and Ronald. Ronald had access so that he could remotely fix the rides when they went down. There was also a computer in Ronald's house linked to the mainframe. This worried Maddox slightly and he even thought of disabling his brother's account but he decided that he wouldn't. After all what could he do if he was on a cruise ship? If he even went at all.

When the main screen had loaded Maddox had a choice of five menus. One was Barcode Scanner Reset and configuration, Guest or system, the second was administrative options, the third was Rides, the fourth exterior illuminations and park lights, and the fifth the Hotel. If Maddox had selected hotel he would have been able to increase the heat or turn down the air-conditioning in the whole of the hotel or just in specified rooms. He would also have been able to dim the lights or turn on lamps, but Maddox didn't think that freezing the guests to death would help him with his "abominable sister" problem. Instead he chose administrative options. From the sub menu he chose programming and designing, then he chose credits. The ten people that had worked on the programming were displayed in different colors. Maddox's eyes skimmed through the list and about half way down he found what he hoped he wouldn't. The same Samantha Lewis reflected in Maddox's bright blue eyes. His stomach plummeted. Benny swore and Oliver totally oblivious to what was happening around him carried on typing.

# Chapter Fifteen

## The Report on SHHTVN

Maddox, his heart lower than his feet got up and left the control room. He was afraid that his sister had worked on the computers however he never really thought that it was going to be true. Maddox didn't feel like going on SHHTVN to do his report on The Grand Prize Draw, but when he thought of the evilness and malice that his sister had against him he suddenly went very cold and was filled with a certain urge and importance. Maddox took a left when he got to the fork in the corridor, instead of taking the right back to the limo. Down the corridor, through the double glass doors, across the courtyard and into the studio.

"Mr. Lewis what a surprise" said one of the studio crews.

Maddox walked over to Brit who was sitting in his director's chair. Maddox tapped his shoulder and he turned around.

"Hey Maddox what's up?" he asked.

"I'm going to have a prize draw where people buy tickets and enter to win $1,000,000." Maddox said. However he didn't tell him why he was having the draw because he didn't trust anyone at this point. Some people may call it paranoia but Maddox called it 'Being Cautions' If Brit was in contact with Samantha the whole plan could be ruined.

The studio crew prepared Maddox for his speech and as he sat behind the reporter's desk he was unfortunately reminded of the time when he had to sit behind it and tell the people of the state that there were two people missing.

"You're live in 5.....4....3...2.."

"Good afternoon and thank you for watching SHHTVN. Today I have a special announcement. I am hosting a Grand Prize Draw where people can buy tickets and enter to win $1,000,000. The tickets cost $10 and are on sale in any gas station, Wal-mart, Publix or Win Dixie in Orange, Flagler, Volusia, and Osceola counties for more information please see the advertisement that is being published in The Daily Post tomorrow." Maddox paused and then said "Participants will be required to fill in an information sheet with their name, address and phone number so that they may be contacted if they are the lucky winner. Thank you for listening Ladies and Gentlemen, good luck and have a good afternoon."

"Cut" Brit yelled. The moment that he said it the light atop the camera that was filming Maddox went out and the TV screen in the Studio displayed "A Haunted Movie" (Spooky Studios latest production). Maddox thanked the crew and left the studio with Benny.

He went across the courtyard and through the door as if he were going back to the limo. He then turned right and went through a door. He found himself in a room that was full of office cubicles. Each had a numbers on. They were all very small with just enough room for a desk, two chairs and a computer. Maddox headed for his wife's cubical number which was 666. They had always joked about her cubical number. There wasn't 666 cubicles in the accounting office and the reason that they numbers were so high was because they started at 600. As the billionaire headed to his wife's cubical he heard snippets of what the occupants were saying into their telephone receiver.

Maddox poked his head over the low partition of the cubical and said,

"Hi Honey" Suzy jumped and then said

"Hey Maddy" She grinned up at him.

"Guess who I had another visit from this morning?"

"Oh Maddox not again. You really are going to have to do something about your sister."

"Funny you should say that actually because just as Samantha was leaving the detectives that are working on the disappearances came to pay me a visit. They needed to talk to Ronald and Samantha but as Ronald has gone on that cruise and I don't even know where Samantha is living I couldn't help them. They did however come up with a way for me to find out but it's going to cost me a million dollars. Which if it catches her, I don't mind spending."

"Ok are you going to tell me what it is then?"

"I'm going to have a Grand Prize Draw. People can buy tickets for ten dollars and the winner will take home a million dollars. They will have to fill out an information sheet before they can buy a ticket. The excuse I gave for that was so that they can contact if they are the winner."

That's a very good idea and I bet it'll work." Suzy said.

"Right, well I had better get back to the office, I'll speak to you when I get home, and I should be home by about five. Love you"

"You too" she replied. Maddox kissed his wife and left. He met Benny who waiting for him outside the door.

On the way back to the Champs building Maddox was wondering if his plan to trap his sister could ever work. He hoped it would because if it didn't he would have to close Spooky Hollow completely.

# Chapter Sixteen

## The Grand Prize Draw

The next day was Saturday so neither Paul nor Misty had school. Maddox and Suzy were also off work. Maddox was first to get up as usual. He made himself a cup of coffee and poured himself a bowl of Rice Krispies. While he sat at the table chomping on his breakfast he heard a clonk outside so he got up and went out to see what it was. Maddox saw that "The Daily Post" (Their subscribed newspaper) was laying on the front of his car.

"Oi" yelled Maddox to the newspaper boys retreating back. As he didn't get a response he picked up the newspaper from the front of the car and went back into the house. Maddox retrieved his coffee and what was remaining of his breakfast and went into the living room where he perched himself in his favourite arm chair and put his feet up on the black leather stool. Just as he had unrolled the paper and started to scan the front page, there was the sound of bare feet coming down the oak stairs. Suzy finished her descent of the stairs and followed the corridor to the living room where she thought her husband would be. Maddox looked up from the paper and said,

"Well good morning sleepy head"

"Good morning" she replied through a yawn

"Are the children awake yet?" he asked

"No I don't think so but I shouldn't think that they will be too long."

Maddox held up the news paper so that Suzy could see the front page.

Her eyes fell onto the headline that read Wealthy theme park owner promises a million dollars to lucky winner. Suzy took the paper from Maddox and read the article.

"That'll get Samantha's attention" she said

"Yeah but look what's written below it" Suzy turned back to the front page of the post and read aloud "Four missing people and no evidence, investigators dumbfounded."

"I shouldn't worry about that Maddox, if Samantha reads it and I bet you she will it will just prove to her that they are on her case and that it won't be long before they catch her, maybe it will do some good, maybe she will lose her nerve."

"I'm still not one hundred percent that it is Samantha." replied Maddox "there again I don't really know who else it could be"

"I think that it's Samantha, I mean who else can it be?" The two were silent for a couple of minutes until there were more footsteps on the stairs.

"I best go and make some porridge for the kids." Suzy said.

"Can you tell them that we won't be playing volley ball in the pool today because it looks like it's going to rain." Maddox said as he looked out of the big window over the TV. Black clouds were visible on the horizon.

Maddox sat and read his paper for a while, and Suzy and the kids played scrabble.

At around 12:00 Suzy went and made some cheese rolls and brought them into the lounge. By this time it had begun to rain very hard and Maddox wondered what they were going to do for the rest of the day as Misty and Paul got very restless, very quickly. Suzy however came to the rescue like always, by pulling out the James Bond DVD collection. The whole family was mad on 007. Paul picked the first movie (Die another day) and put it into the DVD player. Misty squealed every time that there was something that made you jump.

After the third 007 movie (The world is not enough) Maddox decided to do some paperwork that he had been meaning to do for a long time. So he sat at the dining table pondering over figures while at the same glancing up at Goldeneye.

At 5:15 Suzy went and made dinner while Maddox (who had got fed up with his paper work) and their two children watched Tomorrow Never Dies.

Sitting at the dinner table that night while tucking into a mouth watering chilli Maddox suddenly had a thought.

"If the weather is the same as this tomorrow which they said it would be, and as it is a bank holiday Monday do you guys want to go to Texas for a couple of days?"

"Yea" yelled Misty and Paul.

"That would be nice, I'm sure that you mum would like to see us."

"Well that's actually what she said when I spoke to her earlier. In fact she was the one that suggested it."

That evening when Misty and Paul had gone up to bed and Suzy had gone for a shower, Maddox called Rupert.

Rupert was the man in charge of the Lewis company jet.

"Hello Maddox" said Rupert

"Hi Rupert can..." started Maddox then he said, "How did you know that it was me?"

"It came up on caller I.D. and can I do what?" Rupert asked.

"Can you have the Jet ready to go at 6:00 am tomorrow morning? And can you also call Darren (Darren was Maddox's pilot) and ask him if he will fly us to Texas and then come and collect us on Monday night around 9:00 pm?"

"Sure, no problem. You going to visit you mum?"

"Yeah, this weather is annoying. I moved to Florida for the sun and look where it got me. Still never mind"

"They reckon that there is a hurricane coming within the next few weeks" replied Rupert.

"Oh great" said Maddox sarcastically.

"Ok well I'll see you tomorrow at 6:00 am sharp."

"Take care Roops. Bye"

Maddox put down the receiver and called Benny.

"Hello" said a women's voice that Maddox didn't recognize.

"If Benny there please?" he asked.

"Who's calling?"

"This is Maddox Lewis."

"One moment please"

Maddox waited for what seemed like five minutes and when he was just about to hang up and try later he heard Benny's voice.

"Sorry about that Maddy I was in the shower."

"Who's that women that answered the phone?"

"Oh that's my girlfriend Alana. So what can I do for you then?"

"Can you pick me and my family up tomorrow at 5.00 am and take us to Orlando airport?"

"Sure I can, going any where nice?"

"We're going to Texas for a few days as we are sick of this rainy weather."

"Cool. Want me to pick you up when you return?" asked Benny.

"That" said Maddox "was actually going to be my next question"

"Just let me know tomorrow what time your landing when you come back and I'll be there to collect you."

“What would I do without you Benny?” asked Maddox.

“Drive yourself” he replied laughing.

“Ok see you tomorrow.”

“Bye”

Just as Maddox had put down the phone Suzy came out of the bathroom in her dressing gown.

“Who was that on the phone Maddox?”

“Rupert and then Benny. I have made the arrangements for tomorrow all we have to do is pack and be ready on the doorstep at 5:00 am tomorrow morning. Benny will be hear to pick us up and take us to the airport. Rupert said he would have the jet all ready to go at six.”

“I’ve been in the shower 5 minutes and you’ve already made arrangements for us to be in Texas tomorrow. Maddox Lewis I admire your efficiency.”

“Yes I’m very efficient I never forget any...... Bother” said Maddox “I forgot to call mother and tell her that we are actually coming.”

“I take back all that I said” laughed Suzy.

After Maddox had called Rita and told her that they were indeed coming and to have somebody pick them up at the airport, he went to check on the kids. His wrist was now extremely painful so he went down and got a head pad from the medicine cabinet in the laundry room. He put it into the microwave for 1 minute 15 seconds. Now with the pain in his arm easing slightly due to the hot pad he went up to bed.

# Chapter Seventeen

## *The weekend in Texas*

"Come on you sleepy heads lets get going" said Maddox as he went into Paul's bedroom.

"But Dad" he moaned

"No buts get up and get dressed or we are going to be late" replied Maddox, he turned around and left to go and wake Misty up. He knocked three times and then entered. He found her sitting on her bed, dressed with a small suitcase lying beside her.

"How come you're awake so early?" he asked.

"I'm just really excited about going to Texas." She replied, smiling

"How come you've packed your case? Mum said that she would do that for you."

"Well I've saved her a job. Come on lets get going" she said, and with that she put down the book that she was reading, picked up her case and strode by Maddox leaving him chuckling to himself.

By the time Paul had dragged himself out of his "pit" as Suzy called it. It was 4:55 am and tempers were running high.

"Right, now does everybody have what they need? Misty you have your case?"

"Yes dad"

"Paul you have your case?"

"Yeah mum packed it for me" he replied

"Suzy you have our stuff?"

"Yes Maddox don't worry everything is in order"

"Ok" he said as he picked up his wallet and watch from the dining table. There was a knock at the door and Maddox opened it.

"All set?" asked Benny. Maddox nodded. He told his family to follow Benny to the limo, while he armed the alarm. Suzy introduced their children to Benny and he gave her a hug.

"Long time no see, how you been?" he asked

"I've been good," she said, smiling.

Maddox joined up with the four after locking the door. Both Misty and Paul were getting excited because neither had ever been in a limousine before.

They arrived at the airport with 10 minutes to spare. Benny showed his I-D badge at the main gate and the guard waved him through.

They saw the jet parked near a hanger that said Lewis Industries on it. The plane it's self had the same writing but in green instead of orange like the building.

"We're going on that" Paul practically yelled

"We sure are" replied Maddox

"Awesome" said Paul who was ecstatic with energy and joy

Benny opened the door and held out his hand so Suzy could easily exit the excursion.

"Quite the gentleman" she said "a big difference from the bully that I used to know at school" Benny grinned.

Paul ran over to where the plane was and just stood looking at the closed door as if he was trying to open it with his eyes. At that moment a jeep came hurtling out of the hanger and screeched to a holt in front of where Maddox was standing.

A balding man of around 60 got out and yelled "Hey Maddox" Maddox turned form talking to Benny and said "Rupert, how it going?"

"Oh not to bad, the old arthritis in my leg is playing up a bit but I'll live."

Another man around 40 got out of the passenger side of the jeep and walked round to where Maddox and the other men were standing.

"Hello Darrel"

"Hello Maddox nice to see you" he replied "Well we had better get going or we'll miss our take off spot." He said, looking at his watch.

Benny said good bye and promised that he would be there to pick them up when they got back. Darrel opened the door to the jet and they all piled in. Paul ran over to a big sofa that was in the corner. Misty sat in an armchair near the big flat screen TV that was fixed to the wall and begun to take out her DVDs. Paul was more interested in the laptop computer that was sitting on a table in the corner of the plane. Suzy and Maddox sat on the sofa adjacent to Paul.

"Ok" said Darrel "I'm going to get everything ready to go and I'll tell you when we are about to take off so you can get buckled up."

Darrel went into the cockpit and closed the suede curtain that hid the controls from view. They heard the engines start up and felt a judder as the plane started to move.

They got in the queue for take off behind a large 747. There were three or four planes in front of them but they soon went.

"Ok guys fasten your seat belts" they heard Darrel say over the intercom. The four buckled up and as soon as the last plane in front of them was airborne Darrel cranked up the engines and they were steaming down the runway. Up Up Up they went into the sky, the rain sliding off the windows.

They landed at Dallas international airport and as they disembarked they plane the group saw Rita standing by her limousine. She greeted her family with hugs and kisses.

"Gosh you two have grown." She said to Misty and Paul. Rita then turned to Suzy and gave her a hug,

"It's nice to see you. It's been a long while."

Maddox went over to the plane where he could see Darrel coming down the steps of the plane.

"Thank you for flying us here today," said Maddox

"That's not a problem, it was a pleasure, besides, I need to get my hours in this month as I'm not flying enough."

"Well I will see you tomorrow at around nine pm." said Maddox before departing to meet up with the rest of his family. On the way back to the Lewis Mansion the topic of conversation was Spooky Hollow. Maddox didn't have the heart to tell his mother that he thought that her daughter was behind the disappearances.

They pulled up to the main gates of the house and Rita leant over into the front of the car and pressed the button to open the gates. As soon as Misty and Paul saw the outside of the mansion they wanted to live there.

"Daddy, Daddy can we go exploring?"

"Yes, if you stay within the grounds." Maddox replied.

The adults went inside the house while the two children went gallivanting off all over the grounds exploring.

After their exploration of the grounds, the two children went into the house to find their parents and to get something to eat. They went through the back door and found themselves in a large hall. They heard voices coming from a corridor to the left from where they were standing. Paul nudged Misty and pointed towards where the voices were coming from. Misty followed Paul towards the corridor. They stopped outside a door that was open a crack. The voices were now louder and it was clear that they were coming from the room beyond. Paul recognized one of them as his father.

"Mother I don't want to close Spooky Hollow, but if there are any more disappearances then I don't see what other choice I have." Said Maddox.

Paul and Misty looked at each other, horrified.

"Maddox there must be some way that you can find out who is doing this." replied Rita

"I'm trying mother but I'm afraid that if it doesn't work that I am going to have to close Spooky Hollow completely. If I have to do that, I have to do that, but I can't risk putting innocent children in jeopardy."

There was a slight movement on the doorknob, and Misty and Paul fled as fast as they could.

When they were safely out of earshot Paul turned to Misty and said

"What do you think is happening at Spooky Hollow?"

"I don't know but whatever it is it sounds bad," replied Misty

"I think we will keep this to ourselves." Said Paul "if dad knows we were listening to his conversation he'll get mad."

Misty and Paul went off to finish the rest of there exploring around the house.

Rita called the family together at around 7:00 that evening for dinner and as they all sat at the big long oak dining table Maddox turned to his mother and said

"How are you coping?"

Rita looked quite taken aback at the abrupt question.

"I'm not doing too bad, as well as can be expected I suppose." There was a tone in her voice that told Maddox not to press the matter.

The next day Maddox took his mothers Maserati Spyder from the garage, and together with Paul they went out to some of the wells that Lewis Oil owned. Paul found it all very interesting but put up quite a fuss when Maddox looked at his watch and announced that they should get home or they would be late getting to the airport.

Once again, they found themselves at the airport, saying goodbye.

"I think I will come down and visit you next month, and I am just going to have to ask you Maddox why do you have your wrist bandaged?"

Maddox looked at his wife and then turned to his mother and said, "I had an accident in Suzy's Car"

"Why on earth didn't you call and tell me?" she replied angrily.

"Because I knew you would only worry." Said Maddox.

Suzy gave Rita a hug and went and got into the plane. Paul and Misty followed suit, which left Maddox alone outside with his mum.

"Now listen to me Maddox. If you think it is Samantha then go after her with everything you have. But make sure that it is her before you pursue her, also check out that other person that we were talking about."

"I will mother but for now you just focus on getting over fathers death. I love you very much, we all do, and we don't like to see you hurting like this." Maddox gave her a hug and followed the same path that the rest of his family had.

# Chapter Eighteen

## The Draw

After their weekend away in Texas, the rest of the week went by quite fast and before they knew it, the tickets for the grand prize draw were ready to be drawn. Maddox announced the winner over SHHTV. He also put a small advertisement in the newspaper. The money went to a single mother in DeLand. As Maddox was sitting in his office the phone rang.

"Mr. Lewis, this is Dennis. I have been asked to call you and tell you the details from the Prize Draw Card on a Samantha Lewis."

"Excellent, what is her address and telephone number then?" Maddox replied.

"Her address is 1720 South Amelia Avenue, Daytona Beach. There isn't a telephone number on here."

"That's ok, now I have the address I can find the phone number, Thank you for calling." Maddox put down the phone but immediately picked it up again to call Julie Garrett. She must have been sitting by her phone as she answered after one ring. Before she could say anything Maddox said "Detective, its Mr. Lewis, I have her address."

"Brilliant, ok what is it?"

"1720 South Amelia Avenue, Daytona Beach. I'm afraid I don't have a telephone number for her"

"I'll get a search warrant and we will go over there right away." Said Julie

"I'll meet you over there" replied Maddox

"I don't think that's a good idea" said Julie. But Maddox didn't hear as he had already put down the phone. Maddox got up from his chair and went down to the car park at the bottom of his building and got into his car. He had decided that his wrist had heeled enough to drive. Speeding out of the car park he thought about what he would find in his sisters house, the thought worried him a great deal.

When he pulled up outside his sister's house he was surprised to see that it was not a small tatty house, but a big handsome house with arched windows and beautiful oak doors. The police were already there and they were going in and out as they pleased. Maddox went in through the front door into a big entrance hall. He saw Sam and Julie standing in the kitchen looking at something in a clear bag with a red tab on the top. The red tab read EVIDENCE. As he drew nearer he recognized what it was. It was a park pass for Spooky Hollow. Once again his stomach dropped.

"Found anything else?" Maddox asked the two detectives, who jumped when Maddox spoke.

"Mr. Lewis you shouldn't be here," said Sam

"I know but I couldn't just sit at the office and wait for you to call."

"No we haven't found anything else but look at the date on this" Julie passed Maddox the evidence bag and he looked at the date and time that was stamped on the card. It was the same date as the second disappearance

"We need to find your sister," said Sam

"Well she isn't going to come with all the cops swarming around her house, I guess we will just have to set a trap for her to come home." Said Julie "My guess is that we situate a plain car over the opposite side of the road with two officers in it and then we just wait until she comes back."

Maddox didn't say anything else. He left the house and sat in his car for a while before going home.

When Maddox got home he went straight to his computer and brought up the Spooky Hollow mainframe information window. He typed his user name and password and then clicked on the card scanners. He brought up all personnel entry to Spooky Hollow on the dates of the second disappearance. There were thousands of names listed and Maddox got tired of looking through them all. Just as he was about to give up he remembered the integrated search tool.

He pulled the screen up and entered Samantha Lewis. Her name popped up as entering the park at 8:00 am and exiting at 3:00 pm. The time that she was in the park was almost the same amount of time that Carl, Phillipa, Viki and Cravan . Maddox's head was spinning. He didn't know what to do. His finger hovered over the print screen button wondering whether to press it or not. Something in his head was saying don't but still, he didn't know what to do. The police would want to see the log on the computer system anyway so he wouldn't loose anything by not printing the log out but something deep down, something that Maddox could not describe, something was stopping him from printing the page. Then he was filled with another thought. He thought about all the bad things that his sister had done in the past, and all the things that she had said to him when she visited him in his office. Maddox clicked the print button and got up of his chair to collect the freshly printer paper from the printer. The paper was hot from the lasers fusers. He looked up the fax number for the precinct where Sam and Julie worked. As he inserted the log into the fax machine he still wondered if what he was doing was right. In the end he came to the conclusion that either he sent the paper and tried to save the missing children or he didn't send it and the children would possibly die if they weren't dead already. Maddox pressed the send button and he could hear the fax dialling. He waited for a couple of seconds and then he read Fax Sent, on the machines screen.

The doors to the precinct opened and in marched two officers who had Samantha in handcuffs.

"Excellent work" Julie Garrett said to the two officers who apprehended Samantha Lewis. "Now let's see what she has to say"

She led them into the interview room and took her seat opposite the suspect. She waited for Sam. As soon as he arrived they would be able to interrogate her.

# Chapter Nineteen

## The Interview

Sam arrived roughly five minutes after Julie had taken her seat in the interview room. He sat down in a seat next to Julie and pulled out a set of notes, one of the notes had Samantha's picture on it.

"Arrested at the age of 20 for drug possession. Arrested at age 25 for Joy riding. This rap sheet of yours just keeps going on and on" Sam told Samantha.

"That was in the past I've cleaned myself up now." She replied looking indignant.

"We searched your house and found this," said Julie, passing Samantha the evidence bag, which contained the Spooky Hollow access pass.

"So, what about it?"

"This pass is dated the same date as the time when two teenagers went missing in the park, and you are our prime suspect." said Sam, who was leaning over the table and looking right into Samantha's eyes.

"That was the first time I went to Spooky Hollow and I only went to see if it was as good as everybody made it out to be. I didn't kidnap anybody"

"The time on you ticket and the time on the victims log details are very similar. We also have this" said Sam, who passed the log sheet over that Maddox had faxed "We think that you kidnapped them, hid them somewhere at Spooky Hollow, and then checked out." Julie said. It was remarkable how calm she was.

"I did nothing of the sort. I want to call my lawyer now." She said as she stood up.

Samantha and her lawyer haggled with the police for almost an hour. Samantha insisted that she was innocent. The police released her due to insufficient evidence after what seemed like hours.

Julie called Maddox and told him about the interview.

"Maybe it's not her," said Maddox "I felt so sure that it was her."

"Maybe it is her, but at the moment we don't have enough evidence to convict her." Replied Julie.

Maddox put down the phone wondering what to do to help the investigation. At that moment Suzy came into the study holding Maddox's cell phone.

"It's Samantha," she said in a whisper. She passed him the phone and he terminated the call.

"I do not want to speak to that women ever again." He said angrily. "She is making my life hell and if I ever get my hands on her I'll kill her. I know it's her."

"But Maddox the police don't have enough evidence to say that it is her. I mean maybe she is telling the truth. Maybe she really did go to Spooky Hollow for a day out, and if that's so and it proves to be somebody else then how are you going to feel? You would have been persecuting your sister for nothing."

"I'm not persecuting her and even if I was she deserves it. Suzy you don't know my sister she is one of the most evil women in the world and the sooner that you realize that the better." Maddox got up from behind the desk and stormed off into the kitchen.

"I can think of somebody more evil than your sister" Suzy said to herself as she rubbed the scar on her chest.

# Chapter Twenty

# Another Disappearance

When Cedric and Clive Longby got up on the morning of their trip to Spooky Hollow they didn't think that anything out of the ordinary was going to happen. They had heard about the other four people that had mysteriously disappeared, but like all the other people. They thought that the kids had just run away.

"What time do you think you two will be home tonight?" Denise Longby asked her two children.

"Probably about 6'oclock pm I would think." Cedric Replied

Cedric was the older of the two brothers. He was 19 and his brother Clive was 18. Cedric was tall and handsome with spiky short brown hair. Clive was tall with long shaggy hair that covered most of his face; he liked to consider himself a hippie. They had been looking forward to going to Spooky Hollow for a long time but their family who were not very well off could not afford to buy them tickets until now. At that moment their father, David, came down the stairs.

"Morning" he said to his wife and children

"Morning" they replied

"Have a good time at Spooky Hollow" Denise said "and please be careful on the road on the way down"

"We will mother, don't work too hard either of you" Clive said to his mother and father.

Cedric picked up the lunch that their mother had packed them and they got into the car.

They had three near miss accidents on the way to the theme park, and by the time that they arrived both of them were nervous wrecks. The parking attendant took the make, model and license number of the car and gave them a parking receipt. They went to their allotted parking space and then went to pick up their access passes from the ticket booth. Both of them were nervous as they were worried that their tickets would not go through. Cedric handed the desk clerk the tickets and he scanned them in.

"Ok" he said. "Could you step in front of the camera for me and we will create your access pass." Cedric did as he was told, followed by Clive. The clerk printed the access passes and handed them over.

"You have a nice day now." He said.

"Thank you we will." Replied Clive

They went through the gates into the theme park and both were dumb struck.

"This is amazing." stuttered Clive

The first place that they went to was the Haunted house. They were both flabbergasted at how real the ghosts looked. Cedric decided he would play a joke on the girl that was standing in front of him, so when the lights went out he flicked the back of her hair and then moved over to the other side of the room so that she didn't know it was him. The next place that they went to was to the Ghostly rib shack for something to eat. The sandwiches that had been made for them were lying forgotten in the car. Cedric ordered the "full house" which consisted of a large drink, a large roll and a large plate of chicken wings. Clive ordered ribs.

"Why did you come to a rib shack and order chicken wings?" asked Clive

"I don't know. I just like chicken wings." He replied

When there food came there was so much of it that they didn't think they would eat all of it.

"I wonder how many chickens are eaten every day in the state of Florida" Cedric said.

"You say that every time that you have chicken." said Clive, getting rather frustrated. "Besides, how are we going to pay for this?"

"I got a bonus from work" replied Cedric. They were surprised that they had managed to eat all of the food but both felt completely and utterly stuffed, so they paid and went out into the hot sunshine.

"Ok, I think we should go on the freaky climbing frame and then go on the rattle the bones roller coaster. By the time that we have finished those rides our dinner will have gone down enough to go on the Haunted Ghost Train Ride" said Clive who was consulting his park map. The Haunted Ghost train ride was the main reason that the two teenagers had wanted to come to Spooky Hollow and they couldn't wait to go on it.

The queues on the Rattle the Bones Roller Coaster were very long and it took them almost an hour to get to the front of the line. Their passes were scanned and they got on into the roller coasters seats. They were both avid roller coaster riders and so far all the roller coasters that they had been on throughout their lives had felt very tame to them. The seats hurtled forward and they were off.

"WOW" said Cedric. "That was amazing."

"Let's do it again" Clive said.

"No, we should go on the Haunted Ghost Train ride now." Cedric replied.

They made their way over to where the ride was located and joined the back of the huge queue. The sign that told riders how long the wait was going to be read 2 hours.

"2 hours" groaned Clive. They queued and queued and queued. The line just seemed to go on and on. When they thought that they were getting close they rounded another corner which lead to another and another. Both were getting very tired of waiting and just as they were wondering why they had come to the park in the first place, they rounded another corner. The entrance to the ride was about 10 meters away from them.

"Finally. I never thought that we were going to get to the end of this." sighed Cedric. They had their passes scanned into the computer again and got into the very back cart on the train.

"I always find that if you are at the back the ride feels more intense" said Cedric.

"I actually think its better at the front" said Clive.

"You want to move?"

"No its ok we'll stay here:"

There was a slight judder and the train lurched forward. They went into the miner's village and the people in front of them got scared by a ghost. Cedric and Clive chuckled to themselves. The cart speed up and they hurtled down the mine shaft.

"This is the best roller coaster EVER" yelled Cedric.

It was 8 o'clock pm when Denise Longby started to worry.

"They said they were going to be back at 6 o'clock and we haven't heard from them" she said to her husband.

"They have probably decided to go and see some friends on the way home Denise, I'm sure they are fine."

Denise picked up the phone and dialed Cedric's cell phone number. There was no answer. She terminated the call and dialed 411 to get the number of Spooky Hollow.

"Security this is Ted Layman speaking how may I help you"

"Hello this is Denise Longby, My two sons were coming to Spooky Hollow today and they said they were going to be back by 6. I have called his cell phone and there is no answer. I was wondering if you could check to see if they were still in the park."

"I can do that for you." Replied Ted "What are their names?"

"Cedric and Clive Longby."

"Ok give me one moment to pull up their log sheet." Denise could hear keys being pressed in the background. "I am not showing anybody with that name ever been in the park today. Did they come by car?" he asked

"Yes, it is a blue Dodge Ram"

"and the license plate?"

"P266 MOG"

"I'm showing that that vehicle is in the parking lot. But there is no record of them being in the park. It could be a glitch in the computer system. Can you hold for a second while I call our technician?"

"Yes of course" said Denise.

Ted put her on hold while he called Oliver.

"Have we been having any difficulties with the computer system today only I have a parent on the phone telling me that her sons were in the park but the computer is telling me otherwise. I also have a truck belonging to the two teenagers in the parking lot." said Ted very fast.

"No, everything has been working fine today." replied Oliver

"I have just spoken to our technician and it isn't a problem with the computers." Ted told Denise.

"Thank you" Denise said. She put down the phone and turned to her husband with tears in her eyes.

"They were never in the park." She said.

There was a knock at the door and David answered it.

"This is detective Julie Garrett and I am detective Sam Garrett. You called the station in regards to your sons going missing?"

"Yes officer we did, Is there any news?" he asked.

"Could we come in and get a statement from you and your wife?"

"And that's about all that he told me" Denise said after she had finished recounting to the detectives what Ted had told her.

"We will have the helicopters go up straight away and we will have our officers out looking for your children. But first, are any reasons why they may have run away or is there any friends that they may have gone to?"

Denise shook her head.

"We will be in contact tomorrow with any news that we have. For the mean time stay in the house and keep near the phone in case they call. Also try and get some rest.

The detectives left the house and as they got back into their squad car Julie turned to Sam and said

"It's that theme park Sam. I know it is."

# Chapter Twenty One

## Cameras and Rides.

It had been about an hour since Sam and Julie had left the Longby's house and they were now sitting in Sam office wondering what to do about Spooky Hollow.

"I think that the people are going missing on the Spooky Ghost Train Ride" said Julie.

"How is that possible?" asked Sam.

"Well let's face it. It wouldn't be hard for somebody that works at Spooky Hollow to kidnap the children on the ride. I think we should install cameras at every entrance and exit to the ride that there is and monitor it 24 hours a day. I think we should even have a few officers on the look out for anything unusual while they are riding the ride."

Sam looked at her as if she had gone mad.

"Do you realize how much this is going to cost?"

"Well which is cheaper, the cost of a few cameras and officers or the cost of six innocent people's life." Julie said angrily.

"I will call Maddox in the morning and tell him what you have suggested. I will then call the boss and see if he agrees with you. Personally I think this is going to be a waste of time." Replied Sam. Julie shot him a look that would have made any ordinary man quiver. "I thought you were more focused on the kidnapper being Samantha." said Sam.

Julie wasn't listening. She was already thinking about where she was going to situate the cameras and the monitoring staff if she got the go ahead.

"I think somebody is hacking into the barcode scanners and changing the times to make it look like the children have checked out of the park, when really they have been kidnapped and are being held somewhere in the park." said Julie.

"Do you know how farfetched that sounds?" asked Sam.

"I don't think it sounds farfetched at all. Everything in that park is run by computer, it would be so easy for somebody that has the know how to hack into the mainframe and change the scanners."

"It's possible, I guess" replied Sam

The both decided enough was enough for one night so they went home. Neither of them slept because both kept thinking about Spooky Hollow.

The next morning, first thing, Sam called Maddox and asked him about the idea for the cameras,

"You do whatever you think is necessary" said Maddox "I want those children to be found as much as anybody else does. I am giving you a free reign in my park."

"I appreciate that very much Mr. Lewis and we will do all that we can to cause as little disorder as possible." Replied Sam

They both hung up and Sam turned to his wife and said

"We have a free reign in Spooky Hollow. I am going to go and talk to the boss now and see what he says about it."

Sam left his office and went down the corridor to where his boss's office was; he knocked three times and then opened the door,

"Can I have a minute of your time sir?" he asked.

"For being my best detective you get two." he said grinning.

Sam told James about what their plans for Spooky Hollow were.

"Have you spoken to the owner about this?" he asked.

"Yes, and he said that we could do whatever we wanted to find those children."

"Good, well I'll give you a free reign as well. You do what you think will get those children back home safely."

"Thanks Boss I owe you one."

"You owe me more than one Sam" he laughed.

The detective set about getting everything that he needed, ready for installation. He, Julie and 12 other officers went to Spooky Hollow.

They installed the cameras and set up their monitoring station about 50 yards away from the main entrance, in a tent. After the wiring was complete, all 14 of them rode the ride. They were all on the look out for anything that could give them a clue as to what was happening, but the ride was dark and it was very hard to see anything that could help. Julie felt extremely sick when they got off the ride. The rest of the officers said it was the best ride they had ever been on.

Three officers were to be stationed at the monitoring station when the ride was operational. They had installed cameras at the entrance and exits and some in the lighter parts of the ride. The footage was to be recorded for future reference and if anything looked out of place they were to call Sam or Julie immediately.

A week had gone by and nothing had happened. There had been no more disappearances and the detectives were wondering if the kidnapper had lost their nerve.

"Maybe we have scared them off" said Julie.

"I think we are wasting time, the kidnapper isn't going to strike while we have cameras and officers stationed all around the ride. I think we should stop monitoring the ride. It is possible that the kids have just been running away. It could be a ride in this park but how do you know that we have the right one?" Sam said angrily.

He wondered what to do now. He had spent $15,000 on cameras, and about $12,000 on wages and over time, and he still didn't have anything to show for it. Sam was now getting desperate.

It seemed to him the children running away was a more obvious explanation. If the children had been kidnapped why was it that there had been no demand for money for their return, the fact that no one had been in contact about the disappearances filled Sam with dread. What if it was something more sinister, what if they had a child serial killer on the loose.

# Chapter Twenty Two

# A Death at Spooky Hollow

Not for the first time, the computer system at Spooky Hollow had crashed. Oliver the computer technician was getting very frustrated with it as nearly everything in the park, and at Maddox's office building, was run off the Spooky Hollow mainframe. He had come into work that morning to find 20 files had somehow been deleted and that the card scanners had broken. He went to get himself a cup of coffee and set about fixing the numerous problems that had occurred. The first thing he fixed was the air-conditioning control for the Haunt-Inn hotel. This took him close to an hour.

After lunch he decided to start on the scanners. He hoped to get the scanners fixed as soon as possible as Sunday was a very busy day. He clicked the menu which brought up the scanner log. He was surprised to see that there had been four modifications to individual people's card logs in the past two months. One being only a week and a half ago. Oliver suddenly had a horrible thought. There had been two more disappearances about a week and a half before,

"Somebody has been changing the log files" he said to himself, "But whom? There are only three people that have access to this part of the computer." Oliver moved the mouse pointer to the icon that said modifications. This would tell him whom had changed the log, and at what time. But he didn't get a chance to click, because at that moment a ghostly image appeared on the screen. It was laughing, and then it said "see ya."

Oliver, who was still holding onto the mouse, was electrocuted.

Maddox was sitting at home, with his feet up watching 'The Pacifier' with his family when his cell phone started to ring.

"I'll get it dad." said Paul.

"Thanks Buddy" he replied.

Paul ran into the kitchen where Maddox's phone was plugged in to charge.

"Dad it's a man called Sam Garrett. He says it's urgent."

He passed the phone to his dad and Maddox said

"Hi Sam what can I do for you?"

"I have some bad news for you. There has been a death at Spooky Hollow. Oliver the computer technician was electrocuted about an hour ago."

Maddox didn't believe what he was hearing.

"How the hell did he get electrocuted?"

"Our Investigator said that there was a fault with the computer and the power surge traveled through the cord in the mouse. Our records show that he has no family."

"No, he hasn't. I will deal with the funeral arrangements."

Maddox terminated the call. He beckoned to his wife to follow him into the kitchen.

"That was Detective Sam Garrett. He just informed me that Oliver Barker, the computer technician at Spooky Hollow was killed."

Suzy put her hand over her mouth

"How" she whispered.

"He was doing something on the computer when he was electrocuted. There is something going on at Spooky Hollow Suzy, and I really wish I could find out what it is. Oliver's death was not an accident. I know that for sure.

Oliver's funeral was a week later and only Maddox and his family and a few of Oliver's friends attended. Nobody shed a tear but it was a very uneasy gathering. Maddox said a few words about the work that Oliver had done, and that he felt he was compelled to say something as he had no family to look out for him.

That evening Sam and Julie were driving home in their squad car when Julie said

"I think that somebody at Spooky Hollow killed Oliver and made it look like an accident. I bet he found out something about the disappearances and they killed him to make sure he didn't say anything.

"You thought that the people were going missing on the Ghost Train Ride and we found out nothing there so please don't be offended if I don't take what you are saying now seriously." Julie scowled.

"Well what will you say if we find out that I am right?"

"I guess I will have to apologize but until that time I am going to presume that you are wrong." replied Sam.

Secretly Sam thought that Julie was right, but he wasn't going to give her the satisfaction of knowing that.

While lying in bed, Maddox thought over all the possibilities of how the children were disappearing, and who could be responsible, but nothing came to mind. He thought about closing down Spooky Hollow but after all, the police had said that the children had possibly run away so what good would closing the park do.

Before rolling over and going to sleep Maddox said to himself, "We need a holiday"

# Chapter Twenty Three

## The Vacation and a near miss

As Maddox had promised himself, the next morning he told Suzy that he thought they should go on a vacation and she said,

"Maddox we have only been back from Texas a month"

"So" he replied "After what has been going on at Spooky Hollow I think we need a break. Where do you want to go? France skiing? The Bahamas? Hawaii?"

"I would like to go to Hawaii." She said.

"Ok fine. We'll take the kids out of school for a week. I'll put Lisa in charge at the office, and Ted Layman is more than capable of keeping everyone in toe at Spooky Hollow."

Maddox left the kitchen and Suzy stood by the oven completely flabbergasted at her husband's sudden urge to go on holiday. She was also surprised by herself. She felt a sudden anger towards him, it was something that she couldn't explain, nor did she like it.

As soon as the hotels front desk in Hawaii opened that Monday, Maddox made the hotel arrangements and the flight details. He called his pilot and told him when and where they were going and when they were coming back, he then called his children's school and told them that he and his family were taking a well earned break and that he would be taking them out of school for a week.

That evening when Suzy had picked up the kids from school Maddox told them what they were going to be doing and they were very surprised but they loved the idea of being out of school for a week.

"Your going to have to work extra hard to catch up when you come back, you know that don't you?" said Maddox. They both nodded. "Well it's all set then. Benny will be here tomorrow to pick us up and take us to the airport and if all goes well we should be in Hawaii on Wednesday.

As per normal Maddox was the first up the next morning and he made sure that the rest of his family was up at the same time. He banged on both Misty and Paul's doors three times. He heard Misty groan and Paul yell "What are we getting up this early for?" Maddox ignored him.

He went into the kitchen where his wife was putting on a pot of coffee. He kissed her and said "This is going to be a holiday to remember." She looked up into his eyes and he felt like the happiest man on earth. However, she didn't smile. Maddox didn't notice this because at that moment Paul came into the kitchen in a bad mood.

"You should be happy Paul, we are going on holiday." said Maddox.

"If you think I am happy about being woken up at four o'clock in the morning you're mad." he grumbled.

"Don't be rude to your father" snapped Suzy

"Sorry dad." he said.

They had been up for about 20 minutes when the door bell rang. It was Benny.

"You guys ready?" he asked

"Yup" replied Maddox

Benny picked up the few bags that they had and went to put them in the limousine. The holiday makers followed after him.

It took them a good two hours to get to Orlando International Airport as the traffic on I-4 was very heavy. When they finally arrived, Maddox's pilot was once again waiting for them. They boarded the jet and when the got the clearance for take off, Maddox told his kids to strap in.

It was a long flight and Misty and Paul were getting very board. They had watched all the movies that they had brought with them and were now bugging their father to tell them stories, but all Maddox wanted to do was sleep. The pilot let Paul sit in the cockpit for a while and he was amazed at the amount of buttons, dials, and lights that there was to control the aircraft.

About 7 hours into the flight they all decided that they would try and get some sleep as getting up at four o'clock in the morning was not something that they were accustomed too.

By the time that they woke up there was only two hours left to go before they were in Hawaii. Misty and Paul were gazing out of the windows to see if the could see land, and Maddox and Suzy were chatting about what they were going to do when they arrived.

"WOW" said Misty, as they walked into their hotel.

Inside it was like a giant tiki hut, with marble floors and granite tops for the foyer. Maddox was amazed that it had cost so little to stay there for a week when he saw how up market it was.

They had got a shuttle bus from the airport to the hotel which had taken about 10 minutes. The airport was very basic but the drive to the hotel was very scenic. Maddox was trying to see Pearl Harbour but he guessed that they were too far away. After all, they had never been to Hawaii before.

After checking in, they set about looking for where the room was. The man at the desk had given them directions but they weren't very good and after 10 minutes of searching Suzy had to go back and ask someone where to find it. It turned out that they had been passed it about four times and not realized. As soon as they had unpacked, the put on the swimming costumes and headed straight for the pool.

On the fifth day that they were in Hawaii, some thing happened that cut their holiday short.

They had toured the famous sites and had exhausted swimming, so they decided to go and sit in the air-conditioned main entrance and read or play games. Suzy and Misty were sitting on the double sofa in the foyer and Paul was sitting under a big fan in a single chair. Maddox had gone to get them drinks. While he was gone Suzy and Misty played a number game and Paul sat wondering what school was going to be like when he went back as he would be having different classes. Maddox rounded the corner carrying drinks when all of a sudden the big wooden fan on the ceiling started to sway. Nobody realized at first but as Maddox drew closer and closer it swayed more and more until suddenly it came free of the ceiling and started to fall to the floor from its 30ft height. Suzy froze, Misty screamed and Maddox dropped the drinks he was carrying and pelted towards where his son was sitting. Paul saw everything in slow motion. Maddox leapt at his son and pushed him off the chair onto the floor. The fan crashed onto the chair that seconds before held Paul.

"Are you ok?" stuttered Maddox.

Paul just nodded. He was still in shock from his very near decapitation.

Maddox got on the phone to his pilot immediately and told him to bring the Jet and pick them up. He wanted to get his son checked out by their Doctor as soon as he could.

Suzy didn't know what had come over her. She couldn't understand why she had not yelled at Paul to move. Misty was very shaken up and Paul had not said a word since the incident.

They were back in Florida by the next day and Maddox took Paul straight to the doctors.

"Ummm" said the doctor as he looked at Paul "Bed rest and lots of food is what he needs. Hell be fine he's just in shock"

"Should we talk about the ordeal with him or will that make things worse?"

"At the moment it wouldn't be a good idea. Perhaps in a few weeks."

The two left the surgery and Maddox tried talking to Paul about what had happened even though the doctor said it wasn't a good idea.

"I'm sorry about what happened in Hawaii."

Paul turned to look at is father.

"It wasn't your fault daddy. I should never have sat there in the first place. I've also been thinking. Where do you think all these people that are disappearing at Spooky Hollow are going to?"

"How do you know about that?" asked Maddox.

"I heard Christina telling her friend on the phone about it. She said that they have been running away after going to Spooky Hollow is that right?"

"Not quite. But I will tell you what has been going on. About two months ago, a pair of teenagers disappeared at Spooky Hollow, the police and the parents thought that they had run away, but they haven't been found. I then had those card readers installed. You know which I mean don't you?"

Paul nodded.

"Then about three weeks after that, two more people disappeared. Their log on the scanner said that they checked out of the park, but their car was still in the car park. The police couldn't find any evidence that they had been in the park." He paused to look at his son to make sure that he was listening, and then continued. "About a month after that another two people went missing. Their log said that they never came into the park but once again there was a car in the lot that was registered to them. None of the missing people have been found yet."

"Are they going missing in your park?" Paul asked

"Its is possible but I don't want you breathing a word of this to anybody"

"Ok Daddy I won't say anything."

When they got home Suzy was pleased to see that Paul was talking again and from what she could see, he was quite happy.

A couple of days after they had got back from the holiday Maddox received a call from, Julie Garrett who told him that they had interviewed his brother while Maddox and his family had been in Hawaii.

"He seemed completely innocent and other than the fact that he built the rides at Spooky Hollow we have no other evidence that suggests that he has anything to do with the disappearances. Maddox if your sister is responsible she has been very good in covering up her tracks."

"She always was good at that." Maddox replied. "I was sure that my brother had something to do with it"

"We also have reason to believe that Oliver was killed because somebody wanted to keep him quiet."

"It's possible I suppose but how would they know that he knew their identity?"

"I don't know. The ME has put the death down to accidental electrocution so there are limited things that we can do at the moment, but if we find new evidence we can reopen the case."

"Well you are completely free to search for any clues that will help you in your investigation." Said Maddox

"We really appreciate your cooperation in this Mr. Lewis"

"Please call me Maddox."

"We will have a look around and then call you if we find anything. It has been a week and a half so I hope we can still find something that will help."

# Chapter Twenty Four

## The Confrontation

It had been quite a long time since anyone had seen or heard from Samantha, but that was all about to change.

Suzy was sitting at home on a dark and dingy Wednesday with her feet up. The kids were at school, Maddox was at the office and she was stuck at home with a bad cold. She just couldn't find a comfortable position on the sofa to lie in. One minute she was hot, the next minute she was cold. Her sinuses were blocked, her head hurt and her eyes felt tired. She watched three episodes of Desperate Housewives, two episodes of Law and Order SVU and four episodes of Miami Vice. Half way through the fifth episode of Miami Vice she decided to try and catch come sleep. She felt that she couldn't keep her eyes open any longer. After turning off the television and finding the comfiest position on the sofa to lie in, she pulled the blanket up to her neck and closed her eyes. She fell asleep practically immediately but after two hours of sleep, Suzy was abruptly awoken by a loud banging on the front door. Grumpily she got up from her sofa and made her way to the door. Through the glass side panels she could see the face of Samantha Lewis. Her mood went from grumpy to angry in a split second. She wrenched open the door and through a stuffed up nose said,

"What do you want, and how the hell did you know where we live?"

"I followed Maddox home one day." Without being asked to come in, she pushed by Suzy and went into the entrance hall.

"Nice place you have here" she said.

"It was until you came in" replied Suzy angrily

"Now now my dearest sister in-law, there is no need to be like that towards me is there."

Suzy muttered something that Samantha didn't hear.

"What are you doing here anyway?" she asked

"I came to see if Maddox was around."

"Well does it look like his Ferrari is in the drive" asked Suzy sarcastically.

"Look Suzy, I don't like you anymore than you like me so why don't you just swallow some of your Lewis pride and tell me where Maddox is."

Samantha had never been on the bad side of her sister in-law but that was about to change when Suzy clenched her fist and punched her in the face so hard that her hand made a horrible bang when it hit

Samantha's cheek. A man would have been proud of the punch that Suzy had administered.

"You Bitch" yelled Samantha, when she had recovered from the shock and the pain. She returned the punch with equal power and within seconds the two women were wrestling around on the floor, both hitting every part of each others body they could find. Samantha was pulled abruptly off of Suzy by Maddox who had just come through the door. Neither of them heard him enter.

"What is going on here?" he yelled at both women. Neither answered. "Samantha, get the hell out of my house before I throw you out."

"But Maddox" she started

"GET OUT"

She turned and left slamming the door behind her. Maddox helped his wife up.

"What happened?" he asked calmly.

"I was sleeping when there was a bang on the door. I got up to see who it was and when I saw it was Samantha, I opened the door and asked her what she wanted. She said she had come to talk to you. I told her you weren't here and then she said something to me that I didn't like. She wound me up so badly that I just snapped. I hit her and she hit me back and then before I knew it she was wrestling me to the floor and we were hitting each other over and over."

"Well I don't blame you for hitting her; I just want to know why she came here to speak to me when she knows that I work at the office in the week."

Suzy had a cut on her forehead from where Samantha's ring had caught her; she also had a bleeding nose. Maddox went to get the first aid kit out of the kitchen and when he came back he said

"I must say, Samantha looked a lot worse than you do." They both laughed very hard.

"I am amazed she didn't flatten me the way I feel at the moment. I am so bunged up."

"You'll be fine" said Maddox "We have to think of something to tell the kids when they ask why you have a plaster on your head and a bruised cheek."

"We could say that I walked into a door." said Suzy suggestively.

"That might work; anyway I've got something to tell you. I spoke to an old friend of mine from college today and he said that we should get together some time so I asked him if he and his family were doing anything at the weekend and he said no so I have invited him, his wife, and his three children over on Saturday. Is said alright with you?" he asked

"Yes it's fine as long as I can get rid of this cold by then."

By Friday, Suzy felt much better and she started to plan what she was going to do for dinner. In the end she thought that they would have a Bar B Que out by the pool. She looked through her recipe books for an idea for dessert; she stumbled upon a strawberry flan and decided she would make that.

# Chapter Twenty Five

# Josh, Ben and Angelina

It was Saturday morning and Suzy was running around like a headless chicken, trying to get everything ready for the bar-b-que. Their guests were arriving at noon and she wanted to have everything ready by 11:30 so it gave her time to have a shower before they arrived. Although Suzy didn't show it very much, she had a very compulsive side to her when she was entertaining guests. Everything had to be perfect and if even a towel was not put on the rail straight she would get very uptight. Maddox was still in bed, and Misty and Paul were playing racing games on Paul's Playstation. Suzy went upstairs to wake up Maddox, tell Paul and Misty to get ready, and have a shower. When she poked Maddox awake he grumbled and said

"What's going on, why you waking me?"

"Because our guests our arriving in about 15 minutes and you need to be dressed." replied Suzy.

By the look on Maddox's face, he had forgotten all about the bar-b-que even though Suzy had mentioned it about five times the day before.

They showered and dressed as quickly as possible, and just as they were going down the stairs the door bell rang. Maddox answered it.

"Hi, you found the house ok then" said Maddox

"Yes we did, your directions were very good. I hope your don't mind, but we brought one of my sons friend with us, only his parents had to go out on short notice."

"No that's fine, more the merrier, we've got plenty of food so that won't be a problem." Maddox beckoned them in and introduced them to his wife and children.

"Pleased to meet you" said Michael. "This is my wife, Edy, our son, Ben, our daughter, Angelina, our other daughter Jennifer, and Ben's friend, Josh"

Maddox and Michael went into the living room, Edy and Suzy went into the kitchen, and Misty, Paul, Josh, Ben, Angelina and Jennifer went outside.

"Wow, nice pool" said Josh. Josh was about 6ft tall with blonde hair. He was 18 and resembled Orlando Bloom.

"You guys want to play water ball?" asked Misty.

They were all in agreement so Misty and Paul went to put on their swimming costumes. Maddox had told Michael that they had a pool and that his children were welcome to bring their trunks and go swimming, and that's exactly what they had done. By the time Misty and Paul had come back down clothed in their swimming attire; Josh, Ben and Angelina were already in the pool.

Maddox and Michael were talking about what kind of work Michael was in, and Suzy and Edy were talking about their favourite things to cook. Both parents could see their children playing in the pool from the kitchen window.

"The real reason that Josh came with us to day is because his mum is an alcoholic, she is constantly drunk and Josh's dad left when he was five and he had been under the care of his mother ever since. He spends most of his time round our house with Ben and Angelina because his mum beats him so badly when she is drunk. As you can see he is very muscular but he doesn't retaliate." said Edy. "Poor kid, I really feel for him, he hasn't had it easy, Michael and I were going to adopt him at one point but his mum said that she would clean up her act and come off the booze. She never did though"

"That's dreadful" said Suzy "Can't the police do anything about it?"

"They could if he would tell them what's going on. He wouldn't even tell us. He came round the house one night with a bloody nose and a bruised eye and told us that he had walked into a door, we eventually forced what had happened out of him" Edy looked out the window and saw the six of them playing in the pool. She sighed and turned away.

At about one o'clock, Maddox fired up the bar-b-que and Suzy brought out the meat. It didn't take long to cook and before they knew it they were all sitting down at the long garden table munching on a delicious meal. They didn't have enough outside chairs for everyone so Josh went and brought some from the breakfast room.

After the meal the adults went inside to talk about a business venture that Maddox and Michael were going to go into. Paul and Misty had asked if Jennifer, Josh, Ben and Angelina would like to go and play a game on Paul's Playstation. Jennifer had said yes so she followed Misty and Paul into the house. Josh, Ben and Angelina were left outside by the pool.

"There is something about Mrs. Lewis, which makes me fell warm inside. Like when you get into a warm bath. Her voice is just full of love." Said Josh.

"Yes I thought that also" said Angelina "Its not easy for you is it Josh? I mean your mum being the way she is."

"No" he replied "It's not, but I feel like you and Ben are more family than friends because we have spent so much time together. Your parents have been really great too and I am very thankful for that.

All three of them grinned.

"I think we should go to Spooky Hollow" said Josh "If we mention it to Maddox we should get in free."

That evening before they left the Lewis's house, Josh told Maddox that he Jennifer, Ben, Angelina, and Jennifer's friend were planning to go to Spooky Hollow. He asked him what rides he recommended.

"I like the Rattle the Bones Roller Coaster and the Spooky Ghost Train ride. Wait here a minute." Maddox said. He went into the study and turned on his computer. Accessing the mainframe at Spooky Hollow, he selected the print ticket option and requested seven tickets to be sent to the printer. The light blinked and the printer sprung into life. He signed the pages and went back into the entrance way where his guests were getting ready to depart.

"Here are seven free tickets to Spooky Hollow. Just present them at the gate and the clerk will give you your passes. Also here are VIP cards which will allow you to get to the front of every ride in the park.

"Thanks Mr. Lewis" said Josh

"Thank you for a wonderful day Maddox" said Michael, who shock Maddox's hand. He then turned to Suzy and said "the food was excellent, you excelled yourself"

"Why thank you Michael, I'm glad you enjoyed it."

Maddox and Suzy walked them to their car and said another goodbye.

# Chapter Twenty Six

## The Last Disappearance

Josh, Ben and Angelina decided that they would go to Spooky Hollow the Saturday after the meal at the Lewis's house. They asked Ben and Angelina's parents if they would like to come and they said yes. Angelina asked Jennifer if her and her friend wanted to come as well and she was delighted.

The next day was Saturday and everybody was racing around like mad to get everything ready for their day out. Josh and Lucy, Jennifer's friend, had stayed over the night before so that they could get an early head start. Angelina fed their three kittens, Garfield, Blake, and Snowy while everyone else grabbed something to eat. They had all got up at 7.00 am so that they could get on the road by 8:00 am but at 8:15 they were still standing in the kitchen. Angelina was fussing about what her hair looked like, and Michael was frantically looking for the keys to his car. He eventually found them between the cushions on the Sofa. Edy said that she would take Ben, Angelina, Jennifer, and Lucy in her car. Josh went with Michael. They all walked outside together and the four kids and Edy got into her Porsche Cayenne. Josh meanwhile got into Michael's Porsche Boxster. The Webbers had a lot of money but they weren't the snobbish type.

There had been a reason that Edy had asked Josh to go with Michael and that was because both Edy and Michael had decided that the abuse had to stop.

As they drove down I-4 Michael said

"She hit you again yesterday didn't she? That's where that bruise on your cheek came from"

"Yes she did." he replied, looking out of the window.

"You are quite welcome to stay with us as long as you liked, you know that don't you?"

"I know that I am always welcome at your house but I feel like I am intruding when I am there though."

"Nonsense, you are like a second son to Edy and I. When you are not at our house we are always worrying about what could be happening with your mother."

"I appreciate your thoughtfulness, I really do"

They both smiled. Michael pulled of the road and put the top down. The air rushing through their hair was very refreshing. Upon arriving at Spooky Hollow, they had their cars checked into the lot and the parking attendant was more interested in Michael's Boxster than he was about the other customers waiting behind him.

"How much do they run at?" he asked

"More than you make in two years" replied Michael, who was grinning. Just as the attendant asked how much horse power it had, the person behind Michael pipped his horn as if to say "Get a move on." Michael did as he was told, and followed his wife into the main car park. They were able to park right next to each other.

"This Parking system they have here is excellent. They should have this in every theme park." said Michael.

"I think it was Suzy's idea." replied Edy.

They gave the clerk at the desk their tickets and he took their pictures for the security cards. It took them about five minutes to get the cards and they were all getting restless because they wanted to get into the park and enjoy their day.

"Ok, your all set just go through those double gates and have a fun and spooky day."

"Thank you" said Michael.

They walked over to the gates and Michael gave them all their passes. The first place that they went to was the information hut to get a park map. Michael said that they should all stay together while in the park.

"If any of us get separated I think we should meet up at the main gate." All were in agreement. They all argued over which ride they wanted to go on first.

"Hey" yelled Edy "We have VIP cards to get to the front of every ride, remember, so we can do all the rides that you want to without having to wait so stop arguing." They all shut up.

"I think we should go on the Rattle the Bones Roller Coaster first and then the Spooky Ghost Train Ride" said Josh.

So they followed the signs to the Rattle the Bones Roller Coaster and with the passes jumped straight to the front of the line, There were people making noises and rude gestures because the Webbers were getting to the front and the other people had to wait in line for a couple of hours.

When they got of the ride they all thought that it was amazing.

"The special effects were awesome" said an excited Jennifer

"You wait until we go on the Spooky Ghost Train Ride" said Angelina "I've heard that they are so advanced that film makers have been trying to hire they man that developed the effects here."

Once again they followed the signs. This time to the Ghost Train Ride. They used their passes to get to the front of the line but this time they were not met by snide comments or rude gesticulations.

"How many?" asked the ride manager

"Seven" replied Michael

"Ok one person in that kart there. And then fill in behind them."

Michael sat in the front kart with a teenager, Edy and Angelina in the kart behind them, Josh and Ben behind them and then Jennifer and Lucy in the last kart. The ride ground into life they bumped off into the tunnel. Lucy and Jennifer were scared to start but as the ride continued they got more and more confident. As the kart went down the dip into the mine, everyone screamed. After the second dip, Jennifer and Lucy stopped screaming. The train pulled into the station and the lap bars went up. Edy was the first to get out and when she saw that the kart at the back was empty she screamed.

The ride was shut down, the police called, Maddox called, and the staff were put on alert. Michael and Edy went down to the police station.

"Enough is enough" Sam said to Maddox when he arrived. I'm shutting this ride down permanently"

"I think that is what we are going to have to do." replied Maddox.

At that moment, Sam's cell phone rang.

"Sam it's me Julie. Edy Webber has just had a heart attack and has been rushed to Orlando Hospital."

Sam swore.

"Ok I'll inform the children; can you phone up the parents of Lucy Mayer and tell them what has happened. In the meantime you get over to the hospital and keep me up to date on what is going on." He terminated the call and turned to Maddox. "There is nothing you can do so I would advise you to go home" Sam made his way over to the Haunt-Inn Hotel to inform the children of what had happened. Maddox did as he was told. After all, there wasn't anything he could do.

Sam told the teenagers what had happened and assured them that the Police were doing everything they could to find their sister and her friend. He booked them into the most expensive suite in the hotel and told them to stay there until there was any news. The reluctantly said that they would stay. Sam left and Josh turned to Ben and Angelina.

"There is something going on in this park. I am pretty sure that those people who were mentioned on the news went missing on the Ghost Train Ride. They didn't run away, that, I'm certain of.

The police continued to search the ride and the park but they couldn't find anything linking to the children. At 10.00 PM they left the park. Sam phoned the other precincts and told them that the search was going to continue tomorrow.

# Chapter Twenty Seven

## The Ghost of Spooky Hollow

That night Maddox was working late in his office doing paperwork when there was a buzz on his intercom.

"Sorry to disturb you Maddox but there is a Jason Edmonds here to see you" Maddox was puzzled. He didn't know any body called Jason Edmonds

"Send him in Lisa" he replied

The door opened and Lisa entered followed by a very elderly man who was being helped to walk by a young and very pretty women.

"Thank you Lisa" Maddox said. She closed the door. "Please have a seat" he said to the gentleman and the lady with him.

"My names Judy" said the lady shaking Maddox's hand. "And this is my grandfather, Jason"

"Please to meet you both" replied Maddox. "So what can I do for you?" he asked

"I have come to tell you something Mr. Lewis" he said in a very wheezy voice. "Along time ago I used to be a miner in Bagshot quarry where you now have your theme park" he paused to cough. "I have also heard about the mysterious disappearances that have been happening there." He paused and coughed again. Maddox was listening attentively. Judy seemed to have heard the story before and was looking out of the window behind Maddox's desk.

"There were about 50 of us miners and we all used to get together and talk at lunch time. But there was one man who was the meanest and most selfish man that ever lived. He never used to talk to anyone and would always go out of his way to make peoples lives hell. Anyway one day there was an accident and one of the other miners was killed. Everybody knew that it was down to Benjamin but nobody was able to prove it." He coughed again. "The miners including myself made his life hell. But one day we went too far and he committed suicide. However in his suicide note he wrote that his soul would never leave the mine and that he would haunt everyone and everything that set foot in Bagshot quarry. Now Mr. Lewis the thing that concerns me is the fact that your theme park is now built on the very foundations and mines of Bagshot quarry. The Spooky Ghost train ride is in exactly the same place where Benjamin Garnett killed himself."

Maddox froze. He was not the superstitious type but he could not over look the possibility that there was maybe supernatural activity at work in his theme park.

"Thank you for telling me this Mr. Edmonds" Maddox stuttered

"I know what is probably going through your head at the moment Mr. Lewis but I did not make this story up and neither do I want money from you, I just thought that you should probably know."

"Mr. Edwards I do not think that you made that story up. But why didn't you come to me sooner?" Maddox asked

"Because I didn't think that it could be possible that the man that once made peoples lives hell when he was living was continuing to destroy people's lives even after he was dead, and there is one more thing Mr. Lewis. His body was never found."

Maddox stomach did a violent somersault. The man muttered to his granddaughter and she helped him to his feet. Maddox rose as well.

"Here is my number Mr. Lewis" he said passing Maddox a card "Please keep me informed."

"I will, and thank you again Mr. Edmonds." Maddox said.

He flopped back into his chair and after five minutes of thinking of what to do he beeped his secretary.

"Lisa" he said "Can you get me the plans for Spooky Hollow out of the vault please and would you also get the architectural drawings and mechanical diagrams for the Spooky Ghost Train ride"

"Will do" she said

Maddox had a hunch as to what was happening but he prayed to god that he was wrong.

Lisa came trotting into Maddox's office five minutes later carrying a big roll of paper.

"Lisa would you be willing to stay here and help me tonight? I'll pay you" Maddox asked

"Of course I'll stay but you don't need to pay me. Maddox what did those people want if you don't mind me asking."

Maddox told her what he had said and she sunk into one of the leather chairs that were in front of his desk.

"But why did you want the plans?" she asked.

"Because I want to see if there is anything abnormal about them."

"But you brother designed everything didn't he"

"Yes and that's what bothers me" he said. "Ok now what I want you to do is to look for anything that you think looks unusual, such as a entrance to the ride any where other than the service areas and the main entrance. Also look for any other extended pieces of track."

"Ok" she replied.

They both studied the plans for about 10 minutes until Lisa said

"This piece of track just runs from a brick wall to another brick wall and there doesn't seem to be any way to get into it."

Maddox pulled the plans towards him and looked at where she was pointing.

"Yeah your right, and look at this." He pulled a highlighter out his desk and highlighted the place where Lisa had pointed out the piece of track; he also highlighted a piece of wall near the walls with the track.

"By the looks of things this piece of wall opens."

"And look at this" Lisa pointed out another piece of track. "This piece runs from the main track down to the brick wall. And then this other piece" she pointed to another piece of track the other side of the second brick wall "It looks like it disconnects from the main track and goes through this wall and out the other side." The segments of tracks were labelled 'Service Area'

Maddox picked up the phone and dialled his home number. But instead of Suzy answering the phone it was Christina.

"Christina what are you doing at my house?" asked Maddox

"Suzy said she had to go to Spooky Hollow so I said I would look after the kids for her."

"What the hell is she going to Spooky Hollow at 1'oclock in the morning for?" Maddox asked.

"She didn't say and I didn't ask. She left about an hour ago." Replied Christina.

"Thanks" said Maddox and he put down the phone.

Suddenly a terrible thought hit Maddox.

"No" he said to himself "No it can't be her"

"What can't be her Maddox" asked Lisa. Then suddenly her face fell as well. They both starred at each other for about 5 seconds before Maddox grabbed the keys to his car from his desk door and hurried out of the office door.

"Where are you going" Lisa yelled after him

"SPOOKY HOLLOW" he yelled back. Lisa tore after him.

He punched the elevator call button but it didn't work. So they hurtled down the stairs and out into the car park.

"It'll take her another 10 minutes to get there" he said as they jumped into the car. He started the engine and they sped out of the garage and down the ramp to the interstate. Once on the interstate Maddox floored it. Dodging the traffic he pelted towards Kissimmee. He ignored the horns being blasted at him.

"Lisa" he said. "Get my cell phone out the glove compartment and dial this number. 555-088-3021" she did as she was told and when it started to ring, She inserted it into the hands free set on the dashboard.

"Hello" said a women's voice.

"Julie it's Maddox I know what's going on at Spooky Hollow, get over there right now, I'm on my way there and hurry." He terminated the call and skidded to avoid another driver who seemed to be out for a Sunday afternoon drive.

He looked at the clock. Suzy would be there by now. He sped up not daring to look at the speedometer.

# Chapter Twenty Eight

## The dream

Josh, Ben and Angelina sat in their penthouse suite at the Haunt-Inn hotel discussing the disappearances, but they were not aware that they were being watched. However this was not a normal watcher. Normal watchers used cameras, or windows, but not this one. This one used walls and pictures to survey its subject.

"I think I'm going to go to bed" said Josh "I'm just so tired and if we are going to try and solve this mystery tomorrow I need to be clear headed." He said goodnight and climbed the narrow stairs to his bedroom. The penthouse had three bedrooms a living room and a kitchen. It was decorated in Spooky wall paper and the lights on the ceiling had artificial cobwebs on them. They also made it look like there were spirits floating around. Josh showered and got into bed he was so tired that he fell asleep almost instantly

Angelina and Ben went to their rooms about 10 minutes after Josh had gone to bed. After the last door had closed, the watcher floated out from its picture. It glided up the stairs and down the hall, stopping at Josh's door. It slid through the closed oak door continued across the room until it was hovering above where the teenager lay. It dropped down into his body. Josh started to jerk and twitch. This continued for two minutes. He awoke and screamed the ghost flew up out of his body and through the ceiling. Ben and Angelina came running in the door.

"What on earth is going on" Angelina asked.

"I know how the people are going missing." He said out of breath. "Get dressed and come down to the lounge." Angelina and Ben looked as though he had just told them the world was about to end. "Well don't just stand there" he yelled "Get dressed"

When they had left, he hopped out of bed, and got dressed as fast as he could. He grabbed his torch, pen knife and cell phone which were lying on his bedside table.

He dashed out of the door and hurried down into the lounge. Ben and his sister were already waiting for him.

"I don't suppose you are going to tell us why we have had to get dressed at one o'clock in the morning?" Angelina asked. "And how do you know how the people are disappearing?"

"If I told you, you would laugh and tell me that I was just dreaming." He said

"Quite possibly but if you don't tell me I'm not coming" Angelina said indignant

"Ok fine" said Josh "I had just got to sleep when I started to dream. I dreamt that the ghost of William Lewis, Maddox's late father was telling me where to go and find out how the disappearances are occurring." He finished and looked at his two friends who were staring at him like he had gone mad. There was a pause then they both burst out laughing.

"I'm serious" he said starting to get angry "Fine if you don't want to find out if your little sister and her friend are alive or not then stay here and I'll go on my own"

"No, No I'll come" said Ben rather shakily

"We do want to find them, it's just the way you said it"

They left there suite and descended down the main stair case into the lobby.

Angelina jumped as a computerized ghost floated past her. The trio left the hotel by the main doors and followed the pathway towards the ghost train ride.

"This is never going to work, Josh you were just dreaming" Angelina said angrily

"Shut up and stop moaning, it'll work" Replied Josh his temper now rising.

"Who are you to tell me what to do, and where are we going" she screeched at Josh as he led them off the pathway and into the bushes. The sand was soft under their shoes.

"You are the whingiest girl I have ever come across" Josh said with malice in his voice.

"Hey wait a minute" piped up Ben

"Shut up" Yelled Josh and Angelina in unison.

Ben fell silent. He never was one to get into arguments.

After about two minutes of trampling through the brush and sand it cleared, and they found themselves in front of a red-brick wall with a light on it.

"Why on earth is there a light on a wall in the middle of nowhere" Angelina asked. Josh ignored her and took out his penknife.

He counted three bricks across from the light and four bricks down. He inserted his penknife in the cement between the two bricks and prized the brick out. Behind it was a key hole and an amber button.

"How may I ask are you going to open that without a key?" Angelina said sniggering.

"Didn't I tell you that I was told everything I needed to know? Well I was also given everything that I needed. You remember that key that I found the other day? Well that key fits this lock." He said. He unbuttoned his shirt collar and took off his necklace. Connected to the end was a little green key, which Josh inserted into the keyhole. It fitted. Josh let a sigh of relief escape him. He turned it and the amber button turned green. Holding his breath he pushed it. There was a grinding noise and a 6ft section of the wall slid down into the ground.

"Ok" said Angelina "I believe you"

They climbed through the hole into darkness; the only light was coming from the moon. As their eyes became accustomed to the light they saw silver tracks on the floor. They walked beside the tracks for about two meters. The track dipped down suddenly into the roller coaster. The only way to get down was a set of metal stairs to the right of the tracks. Angelina stepped onto the first step but as soon as she did they heard a grating noise behind them and when they turned to look they caught a last look at the moon as the wall went up plunging them into darkness and blocking the only known exit out. They were trapped.

# Chapter Twenty Nine

## Gas, Walls and Carts

They stood in the dark wondering what to do next when Josh remembered the torch that he had put in his pocket. He took it out and turned it on. Josh caught the scared look on Angelina's face.

"Ok" said Josh "Follow me." He led them back to the section of wall where they had come in and over into the corner.

"No what are we doing" Angelina asked. Once again Josh ignored her. He pressed a button on the floor with his foot and a piece of the floor begun to descend with all three of them on it.

"I really don't like......." Began Ben but before he could finish. The lift had stopped and they were in the middle of a long passage way. The trio stepped off the lift and it went back up to the first level. Josh found the light switch and turned it on. They were engulfed in light and had to shield their eyes until they got used to the sudden illumination before them. Josh led them up the passage way to a door, he opened it and the traipsed in. The room had a wall on the left hand with a track leading from it to a wall on the right hand side. There was also a little brown mine cart that Angelina recognized as being one of the ones that was used on the Spooky Ghost Train Ride.

"Why on earth is there a track running from a solid wall to another solid wall?" Ben asked curiously.

"This" said Josh "Is how people are going missing." He pushed a green button on the wall behind him and the left hand wall opened inward. Josh walked over to the opening and the other two followed.

"You see those silver tracks over there?" he pointed to a set of silver tracks about 5 ft from where they were standing. Ben and Angelina nodded. "And you see those red tracks? Well what happens is when that green button is pushed, the next train that comes round is basically doomed, because the last cart on the train detaches and goes into the room." He went back into the room when they had come out of. "And when this button is pressed." He pointed to another button next to the first "It will open that wall and that mine cart will fly out and join up with the main train. Nobody will have even noticed anything. Then both walls will close and knock-out gas will be deployed from those vents on the ceiling." They looked up and saw what looked like four air-conditioning vents.

"But who built all of this?" Angelina asked. Josh opened his mouth to reply, but suddenly a voice echoed through the room. However it was not her usual calm, caring and warm voice. It sounded cold croaky and full of malice.

"So you've solved the mystery of Spooky Hollow that even 10 detectives couldn't solve. For that I give you credit but now your escapades must come to an end. Goodbye Josh, Ben and Angelina."

The walls banged shut and a hissing noise was heard over head. When they looked up, they saw red gas coming from the vents. Josh felt his eyes hurting. His vision went blurred and distorted. He heard a scream and then two thumps next to him as Ben and Angelina fell to the floor. His head became dizzy. He couldn't hear. He couldn't think. Then he too fell to the floor and felt or heard no more.

# Chapter Thirty

## A kidnapper reviled

The kidnapper dragged Josh, Ben and Angelina into a room about two doors down from where they entered. The eight other victims were bound and gagged and at the moment appeared to be asleep. She bound the three teenagers and left the room to go and get her gun. By the time she got back, all her victims were awake and making muffled sounds. The kidnapper removed the gag from Josh's mouth and they both stared at each other for a considerable amount of time before Josh said

"I never suspected you Suzy Lewis. I didn't think that you had it in you to kidnap innocent people and keep them hostage for three months. Though I must congratulate you on you expertise in kidnapping them and us. Not even the chief of detective could find this, kidnapping device" he still sounded groggily from the gas but the effect seemed to be wearing off at a very fast rate.

When Suzy spoke, her voice was deep and croaky. It wasn't even her voice. It sounded like a scratched record being played at a low speed.

Once again Maddox screeched to a grinding halt outside the main entrance to Spooky Hollow. He lent over Lisa and opened the glove compartment; he took out his gun and checked to see how many bullets he had. He hoped that he wouldn't need any. Then again a mortal weapon would not do any good on an immortal ghost.

They waited for about five minutes before they saw lights coming in through the gates to the park.

"What on earth is going on?" asked Julie. When she got out of the squad car that Sam had been driving.

"I know what's going on in this park. I know who had been kidnapping the children. Come with me." Said Maddox.

He led them down the same route that Josh, Ben and Angelina had taken no less than 10 minutes ago. He could hear the detectives trampling through the trees and brush behind him. Lisa had decided to stay in the car.

When Maddox reached the wall he suddenly realized that he didn't know how to get in, but all of a sudden he had a vision of what to do.

He opened the hole where the key hole was. He pulled his gun from his pocket and shot the control panel. The wall made a grating sound and disappeared into its cavity in the ground for the third time that night. Maddox could hear whispering behind him but he ignored it. Once they were in the dark ride Maddox had another vision. He walked over to where the lift to the second level was.

They got on to the lift and Maddox activated it. They begun their descent, and once they were on the second level they could hear two voices coming from a door on the right about 10 yards away from them.

They all took out their guns.

"That won't be necessary" he said. They ignored him. Maddox pushed open the door and they all leapt in. Suzy was holding a gun to Josh's head.

"Don't move" she said in her ghostly voice. "Drop the weapons and kick them towards me or the kid dies." All but Maddox did as they were told. "You too Maddox. I'm not your wife, I am controlling her. I am the ghost of Spooky Hollow. The ghost that has been possessing her for three months and making her kidnap these children. I also possessed your brother. That was how this device in the ride was built. Neither of them have any control over their bodies or actions while I am possessing them. However, your darling wife did try and resist my hold. You remember the trip to Hawaii a couple of weeks ago when that fan nearly fell on your son? That was me. She soon learned that she can't fight the hold that I have on her, and if she does, I'll just kill her. I also made her change the log for the barcode scanners so that you and those dumb cops thought the kids had runaway. Oliver

Taylor found out about the changes to the log, I couldn't have that so I killed him"

The detectives that were standing behind Maddox didn't know what to say or what to do. None of them had ever been in a position where their victim was being held hostage by a ghost.

Maddox managed only one word

"Why"

"Why?" replied the Ghost possessed Suzy "Well I'll tell you why. I was always picked on and made fun of at school, because I had sticky out ears and I came from a poor family. I thought that would all change when I went to work at this mine, but it didn't. In the end I killed the person that was responsible for the Mickey taking and the rumours about me. Nobody was able to prove it was me because I made it look like an accident." The ghost paused "The other miners knew that they had to do something to avenge the guy that I killed, so one day they decided to set a trap for me. However I was too smart for them. I got wind of their plan and so instead of going to lunch with them like I normally did, I went to the changing room, wrote a suicide note, and then hurled myself down a mine shaft. The reason that I killed my self was because I knew that I could do more damage and cause more misery when I was dead. The miners were sorry that they had ever messed with me. I haunted 15 of them for a while until I got tired of it. I then set about getting everybody out of this mine. Didn't you ever wonder why this mine was abandoned when you brought it? That was because of me." The Ghost/Suzy continued to talk about what he had done for another two minutes. But what no one realized was the fact that there was a silvery thread running from the roof of the room to the floor. The thread was thickening and in the end it moulded itself into a man. By this time Maddox had realized what was going on. He also recognized the person that the thread had moulded into. It was his father.

"This Benjamin is the end of the line." It said.

"William. We meet again" Said the Ghost

"What do you mean again?" asked Maddox

"Son. I never told you or anybody else, but I had an older brother." Said the ghost of William Lewis. "He came to Florida to live with adoptive parents because our mother couldn't afford to care for two of us. I wasn't sad to see him go and I knew that he would never amount to anything. And boy was I right."

"You ruined my life. You are the reason that I had to be adopted. If you hadn't been born I would have been the billionaire by now and I would still be alive." Said Benjamin angrily.

William Lewis's ghost glided towards Suzy and slid through her. She fell to the floor unconscious. Josh backed up against the wall and Julie fainted. There was now no longer one ghostly figure, but two.

The Ghost of Benjamin Lewis and the ghost of William Lewis hovered in front of each other staring. Then without warning, a bolt of lighting flashed through the room, striking William on the shoulder. He returned a bolt with astonishing power.

The detectives, victims, and Maddox stood flabbergasted at the sight at which they were seeing. Lighting bolts continued to fill the room for several seconds more; before William cried "TO HELL WITH YOU" he sent another bolt at Benjamin, which hit him squarely in the chest. He screeched in pain. The ground began to rumble and a giant crack appeared in the floor. A huge red hand came up, grabbed at Benjamin, pulling him down through the crack. The ground stopped shaking. The floor mended itself, and the ghost less Suzy awoke.

"Maddox I tried to tell you so many times but I couldn't. It wouldn't let me; I fought it off for a while but..." Maddox put his finger to his lip.

"We know you couldn't help it, we've heard what happened" He then turned to the ghost of his father. "Is it gone?" He asked

"The Ghost of Spooky Hollow will be sentenced to 20 years in hell. After that time he will be free to roam the earth once again. Now I must go. Spend my hard earned money wisely, take care of my grand children, and take care of your wife now that she is back to her normal self." Julie Garrett awoke and Sam ignored her request for help. He was too busy thinking about what he had just seen. "Have a nice life and remember Benjamin has only gone for 20 years so I would advise you to shut down the park." William patted his son on the shoulder, and vanished.

Sam walked over to Maddox and whispered something in his ear. He nodded. Suzy went over to the kidnapped children and removed all bonds and gags. She apologized profusely to each one and they all smiled at her as they knew that she didn't mean to do what she had been made to. They all left the room and made their way to the exit.

When they emerged into the open air, the sun had begun to come up. Maddox went to his car to see how Lisa was. He found her asleep in the passenger seat, with her head resting on the dashboard. She looked extremely uncomfortable. He woke her up and told her all what had happened. She didn't believe him at first. The two walked to the conference room in the Haunt-Inn hotel where they met up with Suzy and the rest of the people that had been down in the ride with them. Julie went to call all the parents of the children that had disappeared. Sam took Suzy aside and told her that they weren't going to press charges.

"The only evidence that we have that tells us that it was you kidnapping the children is their testimony and as we found out why you were doing what you were we can't prosecute you."

"Thank you officer." she said relieved. She didn't know what else to say. She was so sorry about what she had done.

They all sat and talked while they waited for the parents of the children to arrive.

The Peabodys ran into the room and Joanne screamed, "Where is the person responsible for this." Suzy was about to open her mouth when Sam said "Dead. He was killed down in the mine"

Suzy looked at Sam as if to say what did you do that for. The kidnapped children knew that the truth was better of kept a secret.

The Parents of the other children arrived and thanked Sam and Julie for finding their children. When they had left Suzy turned to Sam and said

"Why did you tell Mrs. Peabody that the person responsible had died?"

"Because if I had told them that it was you they would be wondering why you hadn't been arrested. They wouldn't have believed that you had been acting under the influence of a Ghost." He replied.

Maddox thanked Sam and Julie for all their help in trying to find the victims, and Suzy apologized for what she had put them through. Both couples went their separate ways. Maddox made a speech which was read on the mornings news, that the children had been found in Spooky Hollow and that the kidnapper had been killed. He also said that he was closing the theme park but would continue to run Doxam international as a fully functional airline.

The gates to Spooky Hollow were closed, the computers shut down, and the employees made redundant. Maddox was the last person to leave his dream theme park, and he would be the last person to set foot in the 'Haunted' theme park for another 20 years.

# About the Author

Dexter was born and until the age of 13 raised in Bedfordshire, England.

He has always liked to escape into stories, both writing short tales for his friends and parents, and reading many books.

Spooky Hollow is his first real work and was started when he was just 14, he hopes this to be the first of many.

He now lives in Deland, Florida with his mother, Step father and three cats.

Printed in the United States
48459LVS00003B/62

9 781425 925079